IF TH[...]
TURNS PINK...

BY
CARLA CASSIDY

MILLS & BOON®

To Darlene, the daughter of my heart.
Thank you for the joy you bring to my life.

First published in Great Britain 2004
Harlequin Mills & Boon Limited,
Eton House, 18-24 Paradise Road, Richmond, Surrey TW9 1SR

© Carla Bracale 2003

ISBN 0 263 18231 2

Set in Times Roman 10½ on 12½ pt.
07-0204-39333

Printed and bound in Great Britain
by Antony Rowe Ltd, Chippenham, Wiltshire

Prologue

Be careful what you wish for...it just might come true. The old adage whirled through Melanie Jenkins's mind as, with trembling fingers, she removed the pregnancy test from the drugstore sack.

Six weeks ago she had made a wish and prayed that she'd get pregnant and have a baby. With no romance in her life and no Mr. Right on the horizon, she'd come up with a plan to ensure that she would attain her wish.

Once she took the home-pregnancy test, she'd know within three minutes if her wish had been granted. The only problem was that she was no longer certain she wanted her wish to come true.

If she was pregnant, then she lost the man she loved. If she wasn't pregnant, she got to continue to live with the man she loved but wouldn't have her dream of a baby.

She took the test instrument out of the package, wishing she could go back and change all the rules. But she couldn't. She was the one who had set the rules, and it wasn't fair to change them now, after the fact.

So, what did she wish now? It didn't seem to matter. No matter what the results of the test revealed, ultimately she'd lose something.

"Well," she muttered to herself, "let's see if the stick turns pink...."

Chapter One

Melanie Watters would never have thought about it had she not seen him naked. "Him" was Bailey Jenkins, her very best friend and confidant.

Every day for the past few weeks she and Bailey had met at his pond after work for a late-afternoon swim. Today she was earlier than usual. There had been no school that day. Instead, the day had been scheduled for parent-teacher appointments. By two o' clock Melanie had met with all her little students' parents, and her work was finished until later in the evening.

She'd changed into her bathing suit in the school rest room, then had driven directly to Bailey's.

His familiar maroon pickup truck was parked in front of his attractive white ranch house, but instead of going to the house, she headed for his office in the barn.

As the only veterinarian in the small town of Fox-run, Bailey could usually be found in the barn either sitting at his computer doing paperwork or caring for an animal who'd been brought in to him.

He wasn't there, nor was he in the house, so she headed down the lane toward the pasture and the pond that had for the past several weeks provided cool relief against the unusual heat of early summer.

As she drew closer to the pond, she heard the sound of splashing, but the thick blackberry bushes directly in front of her obscured her view of the water.

She worked her way around the blackberry bushes and froze as Bailey came into view. He stood on the end of a small, wooden pier. His back was to her and it was obvious he'd been skinny-dipping.

The late-afternoon sun played on his broad, tanned shoulders and slim waist and emphasized the musculature of his buttocks and legs. Melanie gasped and ducked back behind the bushes, her heart pounding a strange rhythm in her chest.

She'd always known, someplace in the back of her mind, that Bailey had a decent physique, but she'd never realized quite how utterly fine it was.

"Stop it," she commanded herself. This was Bailey...Bailey, the best friend who had held her head while she'd thrown up when she was sixteen and learned about sloe gin fizzes the hard way.

This was Bailey, the confidant who had heard all

her fears when her mother had been diagnosed with cancer a year ago, a cancer that thankfully was now in remission.

Okay, she had just gotten a startling reminder that Bailey was not only her best friend but pure male, as well. She drew several deep breaths to steady her suddenly racing pulse, then cried out, "Hey, Bailey, are you out here?"

"Mellie…hang on a minute, I'm not decent," Bailey's deep voice returned.

"You're never decent," she replied, striving for the teasing tone that had always marked their relationship, trying desperately to forget what she had just seen.

"Okay," he replied a second later. "Come on around."

She rounded the blackberry bushes to see him standing on the pier, this time clad in a pair of cutoff jeans shorts.

"You're early," he observed as he sat on the edge of the dock with his feet dangling in the water.

She moved onto the dock and sat down next to him. "We had parent-teacher appointments all day and I finished up early. I've got to go back later this evening for several appointments with parents who work during the day."

Had his chest always been so broad with just the right amount of dark springy hair sprinkled in the center? Why had she never noticed before?

"So, did you get a chance to speak with Johnny Anderson's parents about his behavior problems?"

Melanie scowled. "According to his mother he has no behavior problems. He's just spunky and full of life."

Bailey laughed, his dark-blue eyes crinkling pleasantly at the corners. "Did you tell Mrs. Anderson that little Johnny has all the makings of a first-rate criminal?"

Melanie pulled her legs up to her chest and wrapped her arms around them, carefully keeping her gaze schooled away from Bailey. "He's only seven, there's time to save him. I've just decided to commit myself to spending extra time and effort on him even if he won't be in my class next year."

From the corner of her eye she saw Bailey shake his head ruefully. "You have a lot more patience than I do, Mellie. Someday you'll make a terrific mother."

His words sent a swift shaft of pain through her. When? she wanted to shout. When will I ever get a chance to be a mother? She was twenty-nine years old and wasn't even dating anyone.

"Come on." Bailey rose gracefully to his feet and held out his hand to her. "Let's swim off the frustrations of the day."

She allowed him to pull her up from her sitting position, then took off her oversize T-shirt, and together they dove into the cool pond.

For the next hour they raced around the pond and took turns dunking each other. Where always before

Melanie found the afternoon swim relaxing, today was different.

Everything was different because she'd seen Bailey naked. For the first time she noticed how the overhead sun pulled red glints from his dark-brown hair, how his smile caused a dimple to dance by the corner of his sensual lips.

They had been best friends since the second grade, and other than for a few weeks in high school she'd never thought of Bailey as a male...he'd simply been Bailey. But now she was faced with the startling re-alization that Bailey was not only male, but a hunky, highly attractive male at that. And that knowledge was making strange thoughts sweep through her mind.

"That felt great," Bailey said as he flopped down on his back on the dock.

"It did feel good," Melanie agreed as she pulled her T-shirt back on. "So, how was your day?"

"Horrible," he said without hesitation. "My life has become a nightmare ever since they announced at the town meeting two nights ago that I'm the judge for the Miss Dairy Cow Contest."

The Miss Dairy Cow Contest was a yearly beauty pageant held on the Fourth of July during a huge town celebration. "A nightmare how?"

He rolled over on his side and propped an elbow beneath him. "Do you have any idea how many tiara-crazed young women and mothers there are in this

town? I already have a fridge full of questionable casseroles that have been delivered since the meeting.''

Melanie laughed. ''That's not all bad. I'd rather eat
a questionable casserole any day than anything
you've attempted to cook.''

''Ha-ha, very funny,'' he replied dryly, and sat up.
''But, I'm serious, I think this situation is going to
get way out of control. Cindy Canfield brought in her
cat this afternoon, said she thought little Buffy was
depressed, then she spent the next thirty minutes telling me all the reasons why she should be Miss Dairy
Cow. Blanche Withers actually did a dramatic reading
for me in the middle of the grocery store last night.''

Melanie giggled. ''The pageant is a big deal, not
only because of the pretty tiara and all the public
appearances throughout the year, but doesn't the winner also get a car?''

''Yeah, a pink convertible, and there's a thousand-
dollar cash prize, too. High stakes, and already the
eligible women in this town are starting to show signs
of Miss Dairy Cow madness.''

''I guess it doesn't help that last year's winner went
Hollywood.'' A friend of a friend had sent a picture
of Rachel Warner, last year's Miss Dairy Cow, to a
modeling agency in California. The pretty young
woman had recently been spotted in several national
ads on television.

''That's definitely added to the fever pitch this
year,'' he replied.

"And just think, there's still more than a month left before the pageant."

Bailey groaned. "Don't remind me. For all I know at this very moment there's an eager contestant in my bed willing to use her feminine wiles to gain the crown. Drat Tanner Rothman's hide," he exclaimed.

Melanie knew Tanner Rothman had initially been chosen to be the judge of the pageant this year. Tanner, a handsome rancher who lived on the spread next to Bailey's, had dropped out when he'd gotten married two weeks before.

"I met his new wife the other day," Melanie said. "Colette. She's really nice. She's opening a baby shop in the old feed store over on Main."

"I still can't believe Tanner gave up the brotherhood of bachelorhood," Bailey said. He shook his head, then continued. "Next year I intend to suggest to the pageant committee that they choose a married man to be the judge."

The idea that had been germinating from the moment she'd spied Bailey naked began to blossom in Melanie's head. "Too bad you aren't married now. You're not only one of the most eligible bachelors in town, but now you're an eligible bachelor with power. A heady combination."

"You're telling me," he exclaimed. He picked up the wristwatch that was lying on the dock and eyed it. "I've got to get back. I've got a couple of animals who need to be checked on."

She nodded and together they got up and began the

long walk down the lane toward the house in the distance. Thoughts flew through Melanie's head...crazy thoughts.

She tried desperately to concentrate on the scent of grass and sun-baked pasture mingling with early summer wildflowers that filled the air. She tried unsuccessfully to focus on anything but where her thoughts were taking her.

"I know how to solve the problem of the single women of Foxrun throwing themselves at you," she finally said, not giving herself a chance to change her mind about what she was about to suggest.

"And what's that?"

"Marry me."

He snorted. "Yeah, right. Ruin my life because of one stinkin' beauty pageant."

"Thanks a lot," Melanie said, unable to help the small stab of pain that shot through her at his words.

He must have heard the hurt in her voice and he stopped walking and grabbed her hands in his. Despite the fact that he had held her hands a thousand times before, this time Melanie's heart fluttered at his touch.

"Mellie, you know I didn't mean that the way it sounded," he protested, his eyes as blue as the cloudless sky overhead. "And you know how I feel about marriage. Never again." He dropped her hands and continued walking.

Melanie hurried to catch up with him. "But this

would be different," she exclaimed. "For one thing, it wouldn't be forever."

Bailey stopped walking once again and faced her, his features radiating confusion. "What are you talking about?"

"A temporary marriage for mutual benefit." She wondered if he had any idea how attractive he looked with his dark hair wet and slicked back to expose his firmly chiseled features.

However, he stared at her as if she'd completely and irrevocably lost her mind. "Not that I'm even considering such insanity, but remind me again, what kind of mutual benefit this marriage would give us?"

"For you, it would relieve some of the onslaught by overeager contestants. No woman is going to show up in your bed if you're a married man."

"And what do you get out of this arrangement?"

She hesitated a moment. "We'd stay married until after the Miss Dairy Cow pageant and...until you give me a baby."

"Good grief, have you lost your mind?" He turned and stalked off, and once again Melanie hurried to catch up to him.

"It would only be a temporary marriage," she continued. "We'd marry as friends and divorce as friends. You get a reprieve from the tiara-hungry single women in town, and I get pregnant."

"I don't want to talk about this. The whole idea is insane." They had reached her car, parked in front of the barn, and he leaned against the front fender.

"Mellie, I'm not the man for the job you have in mind."

"Bailey, you're the only man in my life," she protested.

He gazed at her with a touch of sympathy. "Honey, eventually you'll find the perfect man for you and get married and have a houseful of babies. Just give it time."

"I'm running out of time," she exclaimed. "And you know my track record when it comes to finding Mr. Right. It stinks."

"That's because your standards are too high."

"Bailey, just think about it." To Melanie the whole idea seemed perfect. "I want my mom to know my child before it's too late."

He looked at her in alarm. "Is her cancer back?"

"No, but there's no guarantee it won't come back. You know how much I've wanted a baby, Bailey. Please think about this. You're my very best friend in the whole wide world. Can't you do this one thing for me?"

Bailey was in shock. He studied the freckled face of the woman who had been his best friend for as long as he could remember, and he felt as if he were looking at a stranger.

"Mellie, you know after the mess with Stephanie I vowed I would never marry again," he said.

She waved her hands dismissively. "Stephanie was

a bubble-headed social climber who wasn't half good enough for you.''

He grinned. "That's one thing we agree on.'' His smile faded as Melanie didn't return it.

"It would only be a temporary marriage,'' she repeated. "And I would never ask anything of you after that. Just give me a baby and I'll go away happy.''

He reached out and placed a hand on the side of her face. "Mellie, you know I would do anything for you. When we were in fifth grade I beat up Harley Raymond because he called you a bad name.''

A ghost of a smile curved her lips. "The way I recall it, Harley Raymond made mincemeat out of you.''

He laughed. "Okay, maybe you're right, but I took the beating for your honor. In high school I tolerated you dressing me up in a monkey suit to take you to the prom. I would do anything in the world for you...except this.'' He dropped his hand.

She shrugged and offered him the slightly crooked grin that was as familiar to Bailey as his own heartbeat. "It was just a thought,'' she said.

Bailey relaxed, feeling for the first time in several minutes as if they were back on familiar footing. "What are your plans for the evening?''

She made a face. "I've got appointments until about eight, then I have to come up with final grades before the end of this week when school lets out for the summer. I'll probably get started on them tonight. What about you?''

"I'll probably eat a little of one of those question-able casseroles, then call it a night early. I've got a neutering surgery scheduled for seven in the morning."

"How about a movie tomorrow night," she suggested. Most Friday nights they spent together, either eating dinner out or going to the old theater in town.

"Why don't we rent one and I'll pop popcorn and we'll watch it here."

She nodded and moved to the door of her car. "Sounds good. About seven?"

"Perfect," he agreed, and watched as she got into her car, the late-afternoon sunshine glinting off her long, curly red hair.

He waved and smiled as she pulled out of the drive, then shoved his hands in his pockets and frowned thoughtfully as her car disappeared from sight.

What on earth had possessed her to come up with such a crazy idea, he wondered as he headed into the barn to do a checkup of the animals in his care.

He and Mellie were not winners when it came to the romances in their lives, but they were absolute champions when it came to their friendship with each other. Bailey would never do anything to risk that friendship. And nothing could ruin things like a marriage.

Twenty minutes ago he would have told anyone that Melanie Watters was the most grounded woman he'd ever known. She was bright, logical and had both feet firmly planted on the ground. But that had

been before she'd voiced her crazy idea about marriage and pregnancy.

Maybe the approach of her thirtieth birthday at the
end of the year had picked her feet up off the ground
and put craziness in her head, he thought as he left
the barn.

He entered the house by the back door and walked
into the large, airy kitchen he rarely used. As a confirmed bachelor, most of Bailey's meals were either
zapped in the microwave or eaten at the local diner.

The only really good home-cooked meals he ever
got were when either his mother or Melanie took pity
on him and cooked for him.

At the moment the last thing he wanted was dinner.
All he wanted was a nice warm shower and to kick
back with a cold beer.

He hadn't been kidding when he'd told Melanie it
had been a miserable day. Not only had he been con-
fronted by several well-meaning mothers of potential
contestants, he'd had to put down a beloved old dog
who'd belonged to friends of his.

He walked into his bedroom and kicked off his
shoes, then walked into the bathroom and stripped off
his still-damp jean shorts. He tossed them in the direction of the hamper, pulled a towel from the linen
closet, then yanked open the shower door and yelped
in surprise.

The dark-haired, naked woman standing in his
shower smiled. "Hey, Bailey, I thought maybe you'd
like me to scrub your back."

"Jeez, SueEllen, what the heck are you doing?" Bailey wasn't sure whether to cover himself with the towel in his hand or cover her. He finally managed to sling the towel around his hips and grab another from the closet and throw it to SueEllen Trexlor.

SueEllen took the towel, but instead of wrapping it around herself, held it out from her. "I just thought I'd show you some of the talent I can't show you during the pageant," she said.

Bailey groaned and quickly turned his back on her. "Would you get out of my shower and get dressed. What on earth would your mama say?"

"My mama wants me to be Miss Dairy Cow."

Bailey groaned again and left the bathroom. He grabbed a pair of jeans from a drawer and went into the living room, where he quickly pulled them on.

A moment later SueEllen appeared in the bedroom doorway. To his relief she had pulled on the sundress she'd apparently arrived in, although the top several buttons were undone to expose her ample chest.

"I've always had a thing for you, Bailey," she said, her voice a seductive purr as she advanced toward him.

Had every woman in Foxrun gone stark, raving mad? Bailey wondered if there was something alien in the air, a weird position of the moon, as he backed away from her.

"I'm flattered, SueEllen, but you need to get on home now," he said. "This isn't right."

"And what's wrong with it? I'm an adult and you're an adult. We're both free and single."

"But I'm not," Bailey protested.

SueEllen stopped in her tracks. "You aren't what?"

The conversation with Mellie was still ringing in his ears, and he grasped at it desperately. "I'm not single…I mean, I just got engaged to Melanie Watters."

SueEllen frowned in obvious dismay and reached for the buttons of her dress. "Why didn't you say something sooner, Bailey? You know I would never steal somebody else's fiancé. I do have my standards."

She tossed her head and flounced toward the front door. She pulled on the door, then turned back to face him with a sly smile. "I hope you won't hold this against me in the pageant. I meant it when I said I've always found you attractive, Bailey." Her smile widened. "And now I know for sure just how attractive you are."

Bailey felt the heat of a blush sweep over his features. Thankfully she apparently didn't expect a reply, with a waggle of her fingers, she disappeared out the door.

Instantly Bailey dropped to the sofa and waited for his heart to stop pounding so frantically. He'd been joking with Melanie when he told her he was afraid some contestant would be in his bed. It hadn't crossed his mind that the oversexed, attractive SueEllen might be waiting for him naked in his shower.

Thinking of showers...he pulled himself up off the sofa, carefully locked both the front and back doors, then headed for the shower once again.

It wasn't until he was standing beneath the hot spray of water that he realized what he had just done. SueEllen and her mother were two of the biggest gossips in the town of Foxrun, and he'd just told Sue-Ellen that he was engaged to Mellie.

He quickly shut off the faucets and, still dripping water, grabbed jeans and a shirt. He had to get hold of Mellie. He had to tell her what had happened before she heard it through Foxrun's prolific grapevine.

Chapter Two

The Foxrun Elementary School was a charming two-story brick building a block off Main Street. For nine months of the year Melanie taught second-graders on the second floor, and during that time the old brick building felt like home.

Her classroom welcomed her with bright colors on the bulletin boards and the familiar scent of chalk and children. As she slid into the chair behind her desk, she marveled that in less than a week's time the school year would be over and the decorations on the bulletin boards would be taken down until next year.

The teachers held two parent-teacher conferences each year. The first was held just before Christmas to discuss what improvements needed to be made and any areas of weakness the child displayed. This conference at the end of the school year was to talk about what improvements had been made and what the parents might want to do to help the child prepare for their next year of school.

Melanie checked her watch, then pulled out the folder for Becky Altenburg. Becky's parents would be here at any minute and they would be happy with Becky's progress. She was a delightful little girl, both bright and cheerful.

With her paperwork ready before her, Melanie leaned back in her chair and tried not to think about Bailey. From the moment she'd left his place, she'd been kicking herself for speaking aloud the nutty idea that had momentarily taken possession of her brain.

The very last thing she would ever want was to do something that would destroy the precious friendship they shared. They'd even gone to the same college together in Kansas City. The only time they'd really been apart was when he'd met and married the beautiful Stephanie.

After college he'd returned to Foxrun with his bride. She'd lasted two months in the small town before hightailing it out of here. But the time Melanie had been apart from Bailey had been the most miserable time in her life.

Still, she couldn't seem to get her idea out of her head. Was it really so crazy? There wasn't a man in Foxrun she was even vaguely romantically interested in, and she hadn't been lying when she'd told Bailey that she wanted children while her mother was still around to share the joy.

The more she thought about it, the more she thought it was a perfect solution for both of them. She trusted Bailey more than she trusted anyone, and she was absolutely confident their friendship could withstand an unconventional marriage of convenience.

She smiled and shoved away thoughts of Bailey and babies as Max and Betty Altenburg walked into the classroom. The conference lasted only fifteen minutes, then the Altenburgs left, smiling proudly with Melanie's words of praise for Becky ringing in their ears.

Looking at her watch once again, she realized she had about fifteen minutes before the next set of parents arrived. She got up from her desk and left the classroom, heading for the gymnasium where coffee, punch and cookies were supposed to be served.

About two dozen people milled around a gaily decorated long table in the small gym. The air was rife with the scent of fresh coffee and sugary baked goods. Melanie grabbed a cookie and a cup of coffee, then started back in the direction of her classroom.

She'd nearly made it out of the gym when her good friend and fellow teacher, Kathy Milsap approached her. "I've been looking all over for you!" she exclaimed as she grabbed Melanie's arm and guided her away from the gym. "Why didn't you tell me? I thought I was one of your best friends."

"You are, and what didn't I tell you?" Melanie asked curiously, then bit into the soft gooey cookie.

"Why didn't you tell me that you and Bailey are engaged to be married."

Melanie choked and nearly spit the bite of cookie out of her mouth. She took a sip of her coffee and stared at Kathy in astonishment. "Where did you hear that?" she finally managed to gasp out.

"I heard it from Teri who heard it from Krista, who heard it from SueEllen at the beauty shop." Kathy's blue eyes sparkled merrily. "So, when is the big day? I insist that I throw you a big shower. Oh, it will be such fun! Your mom and dad must be absolutely thrilled."

Melanie's head spun dizzily and she held up a hand in an attempt to halt Kathy's exuberant chattering. "I've got a meeting in two minutes," she said. "We'll talk later about all this."

She escaped to her room, where she sank down behind her desk in bewilderment. Why on earth would SueEllen Trexlor be telling people that Melanie and Bailey were engaged? Surely SueEllen had simply made a mistake…heard a piece of gossip and mistakenly twisted it into an engagement.

It certainly wouldn't be the first time a false rumor had whirled in the air in the tiny town of Foxrun. In truth, with only two television channels available for viewing without a satellite and only one local movie theater that played really old movies to provide entertainment, the good people of Foxrun thrived on gossip and innuendo.

She needed to talk to Bailey. What if he heard the

rumor and assumed she'd been the one to start it because of the conversation they'd had that afternoon?

She would be mortified if he thought she'd tried to push his hand by starting such a rumor. Surely he knew her well enough to know that if she were going to try to convince him to agree with her plan, she wouldn't be underhanded but would come to him face-to-face.

She'd always been one of those people who thought cell phones were silly indulgences, but now she desperately wished she had one.

Maybe she'd have time to sneak into the office and use the phone, she thought. But at that moment her next set of parents arrived.

It was eight-thirty by the time she finished with the last of her meetings. She left the building and hurried toward her car, eager to get to Bailey's and tell him the latest rumor making the rounds.

She unlocked her car door, then squealed in surprise as a hand touched her on the back. She whirled around to see Bailey. "You nearly scared me to death," she exclaimed. "I was just getting ready to go to your place."

"We need to talk," he said. "How about we take a walk over to Millie's and get a cup of coffee." Millie's Family Restaurant was the most popular place in Foxrun.

Melanie nodded her assent, and together the two of them started walking toward the restaurant on Main Street. As usual, Melanie had to lengthen her strides to match his, and as usual, he was clad in tight, worn jeans and a T-shirt.

She couldn't help but notice how the worn denim hugged the length of his long, muscular legs and emphasized his trim waist.

"Have you heard the newest rumor making its way around town?" she asked tentatively.

"If it's the one I think it is, I'm afraid I'm the one who started it."

"What?" She stopped in her tracks and stared at him.

"Come on, I'll explain everything over a cup of coffee." He grabbed her arm and pulled her toward the door of Millie's.

A bell over the door tinkled as they entered into the warm, heavenly scented interior of the restaurant. It was late enough in the evening that there were few diners.

Bailey led her to the back booth, their regular spot for dining. Almost immediately Samantha, Foxrun's sheriff's teenage daughter, appeared to take their orders.

"Just coffee for me," Bailey said.

"The same for me," Melanie agreed. "Now, are you going to tell me what's going on?" she asked when Samantha had departed.

He leaned back against the red plastic booth and raked a hand through his hair in distraction. "Remember our conversation this afternoon when I told you I was half afraid some Miss Dairy Cow contestant would show up naked in my bed?''

Astonishment swept through her. ''Don't tell me...who?''

''SueEllen Trexlor, but she wasn't in my bed, she was in my shower.''

''Naked?''

''As a jaybird.''

They both stopped talking as Samantha returned to the booth with two cups of steaming coffee. When she left them once again, Melanie stifled a grin with one of her hands. ''Tell me all.''

''It isn't funny,'' Bailey exclaimed with a scowl. ''It was downright embarrassing.''

She tried to keep the grin from her lips. ''So, how did things go from a naked SueEllen in your shower to the rumor that we're engaged?''

Bailey frowned and wrapped his hands around his mug. ''I guess your crazy idea was still going around in my head when I opened my shower door and saw her there waiting for me. I panicked and told her I was an engaged man.'' The blue of his T-shirt intensified the blue of his eyes as he held her gaze. ''Who did you hear it from?''

''Kathy Milsap. According to her, SueEllen told Teri, who told Krista who told Kathy.'' She shrugged. ''You know how things spread in Foxrun.''

''I know,'' he replied, looking utterly miserable.

''Honestly, Bailey, it isn't the end of the world,'' she exclaimed. ''The way I see it we have two choices. You can either tell everyone you're a liar or we can get married and follow through on the plan I outlined this afternoon.''

His frown deepened and he stared down into his coffee mug. Melanie waited patiently, knowing that Bailey never did anything without thinking through his options.

She took a sip of her coffee and tried not to notice the length of his long dark lashes, the attractive structure of his facial features.

There had been a time in high school when raging hormones or something alien had made her yearn for Bailey in a way that had nothing to do with their friendship.

She had stayed awake nights wondering what it would be like if he kissed her passionately on her lips. She'd suddenly been intensely aware of his scent, his strong hands and his broad chest. She had hungered for the touch of his hands, to be crushed against his chest, to taste the heat of his kiss.

Then he'd started dating Marlie Walker, a girl with boobs bigger than her IQ and a reputation for being fast with the boys.

Melanie realized then she would never be the kind of girl to attract Bailey on anything more than a friendship level, and she'd studiously shoved aside thoughts of any other kind of relationship with him. And nothing since that time had made her believe any differently.

All she wanted from Bailey Jenkins was his undying friendship and a baby. She could almost smell the scent of baby powder in the air, and she realized how much she wanted him to agree with her plan.

"There's a third option," he said, pulling her back to the here and now. A smile curved the corners of his lips, letting her know he was pleased with whatever he'd come up with. "We could just be engaged until after the Miss Dairy Cow contest. That would keep the worst of the nutty contestants out of my hair. Then, when the pageant is over, we can break our engagement."

"No way, Bailey Jenkins," she exclaimed irritably. "There's no way you get what you want unless I get what I want. If I'm going to protect you from the crown-crazy young women of this town, the least you can do is marry me temporarily and make me pregnant."

She had that look in her eyes. Bailey recognized it well—the stubborn, determined gaze telling him that to argue with her would be futile. She'd had that same look in her bright-green eyes when they'd been juniors in high school and she'd told him she intended to run against Roger Wayfield, star quarterback, for student council president.

Bailey had tried to talk her out of running, believing there was no way she could win against Roger and wanting to spare her the hurt of a loss, but she'd dug into the campaign with a tenacity and determination that had carried her to a win.

"Mellie, be reasonable," he said, deciding to ignore the fiery light of resolve in her eyes and talk some sense into her. "If we just pretend to be engaged for the next six weeks or so, then my life will be considerably less complicated, and at the end of the six weeks nobody gets hurt."

"The same thing could be said if we get married," she replied, obviously refusing to be swayed. "Bailey, you're my best friend. A little thing like a divorce won't do anything to change our friendship. Especially since we're both going into it with our eyes wide open."

"But you know I had no intention of ever marrying again," Bailey reminded her. "And I certainly don't want a child."

She tucked a strand of her long, copper-hued hair behind her ear and sighed in obvious frustration. "But that's what makes you so perfect. I know you don't want to be a father. I wouldn't expect you to be a hands-on kind of father. I'm perfectly capable of raising a child on my own. And I keep telling you this won't be a real marriage. Nothing will be different between us except—" she looked down into her mug, her cheeks taking on a shade of pink "—we'll have to be, you know, intimate in order for me to get pregnant."

Bailey frowned, looked into his mug, then at her once again. "I know how badly you want a baby, Mellie, but this idea of yours isn't the answer," he said softly.

"Just think how happy your mother would be," she said.

He shook his head ruefully. "Low blow," he exclaimed. She knew how much his mother had been nagging him about remarrying and giving her a grandchild.

"Okay, you win. Forget about it."

He eyed her suspiciously. "What do you mean forget about it?" She had capitulated far too easily.

"Just what I said, forget I mentioned the whole idea. We'll tell everyone SueEllen got it wrong and we aren't engaged, and I'll figure out another way to get what I want."

"What are you talking about?"

Her gaze darted to a point on the wall just over his head. "I want a baby, Bailey." Her green eyes sought his once again. "I'm tired of playing the favorite aunt to my nieces and nephews. I'm financially stable and emotionally ready to become a mother. I'm sure I can find somebody here in Foxrun to be a sperm donor, so to speak."

"Like who? I can't even believe we're having this conversation."

"I don't know why you're so surprised. I've been talking about wanting a child for months now."

"Yeah, but I thought it was kind of like me talking about wanting a Jaguar. You know, it would be nice if I got one, but right now it's pretty much out of the question."

"But me getting pregnant isn't out of the question," she protested. "It's just a matter of picking which man in Foxrun I'm going to sleep with."

"Like who? I know Fred Ketchum has a hot crush on you. Sleep with him and your kid will look like a werewolf."

She laughed. "Fred is all right. He can't help it that he's unusually hairy. But you're right, I'm not sure I'd want his DNA in any child of mine." She took another sip of her coffee, then continued. "But, there is Buck Walton. I'm sure Buck wouldn't mind a couple of rolls in the hay with me."

"Oh, yeah, you'd definitely want his DNA," Bailey said dryly. "If the kid takes after his father he'll be swilling beer by the time he's two and will have a vocabulary of four-letter words that will astound the world."

"Why are you being so negative?" she asked impatiently.

"Why are you so set on doing this?" he countered. The whole discussion of who she would choose to sleep with was irritating him.

She twirled a strand of her shiny hair between two fingers, a familiar gesture that told him she was concentrating. "Bailey, you and I both know what it's like to be raised by older parents. Goodness knows, we've talked about it often enough."

He nodded. It was true. It had been one of their common complaints when growing up. Both Mellie's and his parents had been older when they had been born and they had spent many hours complaining about the fact that their parents were so much older than their friends' parents.

"If I wait for love and romance and eventually marriage and pregnancy, I'm going to be retired by the time my child is graduating from high school."

"Is your sister pregnant again?"

The telltale blush that momentarily stole over her face gave him his answer. Mellie's sister, Linda, was nothing short of a baby factory, producing a baby a year for the past four years.

"Yes, but that has nothing to do with my decision to get pregnant," she replied tersely.

He knew better. He knew that each new baby born into the Watters family had increased Mellie's desire for a child of her own.

Before he could reply, he spied MaryAnn Bartel entering the diner. She was dressed to kill in a pair of tight black jeans and a hot-pink midriff top the size of a bandage. Her eyes widened in delight at the sight of him, and he steeled himself for yet another encounter with a mad cow contestant.

"Bailey," she squealed, her thick perfume reaching him before she did. Her smile faltered as she saw Melanie. "Oh, hi, Melanie. So, it's true? The two of you are engaged?"

Bailey knew now was his chance to set the record straight, to explain to MaryAnn that the rumor about him and Melanie was false. But he saw the light of fanaticism in her bright blue eyes, the tiny sparkles in their depths appearing like tiny tiaras.

He had a sudden vision of his life in the next six weeks, a life inundated with stress because of the stupid Miss Dairy Cow Contest. He also thought of his mother, who had become an irritating broken record on the topic of wanting a grandchild.

A temporary marriage to Mellie would solve a host of problems. There would certainly be no surprises with Mellie. He knew her as well as he knew himself, and he couldn't imagine anything ruining their friendship, not even a marriage, a pregnancy and a subsequent divorce.

"It's true," he said, and saw the surprise that lit Mellie's eyes. He smiled at her, hoping that neither of them came to regret the split-second decision he'd made to follow through on her crazy scheme.

Chapter Three

It was just another Friday. That's what Melanie told herself as she stepped outside of the school building and into the warm late-afternoon sunshine.

It was just a usual Friday afternoon. Bailey would pick her up from school, they'd go to the video store and rent a couple of movies, then go back to his house and eat popcorn and watch the movies.

They had spent countless Friday nights this way, and never had she felt the dancing of butterflies in the pit of her stomach. Of course, never before had they stopped on the way to the video store at the county clerk's office to get a marriage license.

There was absolutely no reason to be nervous, she told herself. This was what she had wanted, and it was a perfect plan for both of them. Still, no amount of rational thought seemed to still the jitters in-side her.

She supposed it was natural. It wasn't every day she promoted the idea of a temporary marriage to a man. She walked to the curb as she spied Bailey's maroon pickup truck approaching.

He pulled to a halt at the curb and reached over to open the door for her. The first thing she noticed when she slid into the vehicle was that he wasn't wearing his jeans, but rather was clad in a pair of navy dress slacks and a pinstriped short-sleeved dress shirt.

Funny. She usually wore slacks to school, but had opted for a dress today. It was as if someplace in the back of their minds they'd decided this day deserved better wear than usual.

"Changed your mind yet?" he asked the moment she got into the truck.

"No. Have you?"

"At least a hundred times since last night," he ad-mitted. He shot her one of his grins that made his dimple appear, near the right side of his mouth. "But each time I decided not to go through with it, my mother's strident voice would fill my head."

Melanie grinned. "And what is your mother's voice saying?"

"The usual. When am I going to get married again. If I'd married a local girl the first time I might not be divorced. She'll be dead and in her grave before I

finally settle down and give her grandchildren." He
pulled away from the curb. "Trust me, Melanie, be
grateful you have a sister. Being an only child can
definitely be a burden."

"What is she going to say when we get divorced?"
Melanie asked, trying not to notice how the sunshine
drifting through the truck window shone on his rich,
dark hair.

"I think after two strikes she'll finally get off my
back about being single."

"And she'll have a grandchild to dote on," Melanie reminded him.

He parked in front of the county clerk's office. He
turned in his seat to look at her. "Mellie, before we
go inside, I think we need to talk about some things."

"Like what?"

"If we get the license now, then I figure on Saturday we can go to Jeb Walker's and he can marry
us." Jeb Walker was the local justice of the peace.
"I'm assuming you'll be moving in with me. I'm not
about to move into that tiny apartment of yours."

Melanie hadn't thought that far ahead. Of course
they would have to live together, and with Bailey's
veterinarian practice and nice ranch house, it made
sense that she would move in there. The thought of
moving in with him suddenly made their plans more
real than anything else had before, and once again
butterflies danced in her stomach.

"I probably should just keep paying rent on the

apartment even though I won't be there for a month or two," she said thoughtfully. "Oh, and before I forget it, Mom called and asked if I'd pick up a prescription for her at the drugstore and drop it by on the way to your house."

"No problem," he agreed easily. His gaze continued to hold hers, and she'd never seen his eyes so blue or so serious. "Last chance to change your mind, Mellie."

"I'm not going to change my mind, Bailey. I'm going into this with both eyes wide open. You give me a baby, I'll give you a divorce. You can have as much or as little a role as you want in the baby's life, but no matter what, we go right back to the way things have always been between us."

He cast her a quick grin. "Sounds like a perfect plan." He opened his truck door and she did the same, trying not to think of the old adage about the best-laid plans of mice and men.

It took them only a few minutes to obtain the marriage license, then they went to the drugstore to pick up Melanie's mom's prescription and on to the video store to rent movies for the night.

By the time they were on their way to Melanie's parents place, the nerves that had been dancing in her stomach had stopped. They had bickered in the video store over which movies to rent, as they did every time they rented movies. The very normalcy of the good-natured arguing set her at ease and assured her that nothing had changed between them.

As they headed down the road toward the Watters farmhouse, they shared the events of their day. Melanie loved hearing about his work with animals, and he listened patiently as she vented about a particular student's misbehavior or extolled the virtues of another student.

"It's hard to believe there's just a week left of school," she said.

"This will work out really great for me," Bailey said. "You'll be out of a job and will be able to cook and clean for me." He shot her a teasing glance. "It's what wives do."

"Wrong century, Bailey. And definitely wrong woman," she replied lightly. "If you think I'm going to spend my time as your wife picking up your dirty socks and recapping your tube of toothpaste, then you have another think coming."

"I knew it was too good to be true," he exclaimed as he turned down the lane that led to the Watters place.

As always a burst of warmth swept through her as her parents' farmhouse came into view. The three-bedroom ranch was where Melanie had been born and all the wonderful memories of her childhood resided here.

"Looks like company," Bailey said, pointing to a scattering of parked cars in the driveway.

"Must be bridge night," Melanie replied. "That's probably why Mom asked me to pick up the prescription. She was busy cooking and cleaning for the bridge gang."

Bailey pulled to a halt. "I'll just wait here," he said.

Melanie nodded and got out of the truck. Before she could reach the house her younger sister, Linda, came out and hurried toward her.

"Linda, what are you doing here?" Melanie asked.

"Ben is working late so I decided to stop by for a little visit." She looked over at the truck where Bailey was waiting. Raising one arm, she motioned for him to get out of the truck, then looked back at Melanie.

"How are you feeling?" Melanie asked.

Linda touched her still-flat stomach and winced. "Okay, but I've already started with the morning sickness. I didn't have it this early with any of the other three pregnancies."

A touch of envy swept through Melanie. Linda had it all, a loving husband, a houseful of kids and a complexion without a single freckle. With her blond hair and peaches-and-cream skin tone, she'd taken after their mother, Marybeth.

Melanie had received their father's genetic characteristics. Walter Watters, better known in Foxrun as Red, had been red-haired and freckled in his youth. His hair was now snow-white and his freckles had faded with age, unlike Melanie's.

Bailey approached where the two stood. "Bailey Jenkins, you know that if you don't come inside and say hello to Mom and Dad they'll be upset," Linda said.

"I was just running in to drop this off." Melanie held up the pill bottle they'd gotten from the drugstore.

"Well, come on, then," Linda replied. "And you, too, Bailey. The kids will want to see you."

Together the three of them entered the front door and into the living room, where a large group of people were gathered. "Surprise!" they all yelled collectively.

Suddenly Melanie was being squeezed and hugged and kissed on the cheek by friends, neighbors and co-workers. Stunned, she realized the crepe paper and balloons weren't for a bridge night party, but rather for her and Bailey.

She glanced over to Bailey and saw the sheer panic in his widened eyes. They had hoped to do this quietly, without a fuss, knowing that it was all going to be temporary. She should have known there was no way to do anything quietly in Foxrun.

"Darling girl." Bailey's mother Luella enveloped Melanie in a fierce hug. "We've all been wondering when the two of you would finally figure out that you were absolutely perfect for each other."

"Lu...give the girl a chance to breathe," Bailey's father Henry said.

"Oh, hush up, Henry. I have a right to give my future daughter-in-law more than a little bitty hug." She released Melanie and stepped back. "I can't tell you how happy we all are. So, when's the big date?"

The entire crowd had fallen silent, and Melanie looked at Bailey for support. He walked over to her side. "We're planning a very small ceremony next Saturday."

"Next Saturday!" Marybeth looked at her daughter in horror. "But that's impossible. We can't do a wedding right in a week."

"Mom, Bailey and I have agreed we don't want anything elaborate. Just a simple ceremony without any frills."

"We'll see," Marybeth replied, and gave Melanie a hug. "In the meantime we've got cake and goodies and a party to enjoy."

Bailey was in a mild state of shock. Although rationally he knew he and Melanie had been fools to think they could somehow sneak off to a justice of the peace and be married, he'd desperately hoped they could have done just that.

But already the potential mothers-in-law had their heads together, and he knew they were discussing color schemes and flowers and all the things to transform a simple ceremony into nothing short of a circus.

He got himself a cup of lime-colored punch and looked over to where Mellie was standing in a circle of women. Her freckles appeared to be standing out from her skin, and he knew she was struggling with the same feelings he was.

In their brief discussions of planning this whole thing, neither of them had taken into consideration that the situation would force them to lie to friends and family.

The lies tasted bad in his mouth, but to tell everyone the truth would be far more disastrous. Foxrun had the moral compass of the fifties, and a teacher of their children involved in a plot to marry just to get pregnant would be ridden out of town on a rail.

"Bailey, my boy." Red Watters clapped him on the back and beamed a smile. "I can't think of a better man to love and honor our Melanie."

"I do love her," Bailey replied. This much was true. He'd always loved and adored Mellie, just not in a romantic kind of way.

"Hell, son. We all knew you loved each other, we just wondered how long it would take for the two of you to realize it," Red exclaimed.

Red spoke with him for a few minutes longer, then drifted off to the table for a piece of cake. Bailey took the opportunity to sneak outside for a breath of fresh air.

Night had fallen, bringing with it a cool breeze. He walked over to the porch swing in the shadows and jumped in surprise as he saw Mellie sitting there.

"Ah, another escapee," he said as he eased down next to her on the narrow swing.

"They're all having such a good time I didn't think anyone would miss me," she replied.

"Yeah, I figured the same thing."

For a moment the two of them swung slowly in silence, the only sounds the laughter and talking of the people inside the house and the clicking and buzzing of insects outside the house.

Bailey became aware of a soft floral scent in the air, and he leaned back in the seat and looked around, attempting to identify the source.

It was too late in the year for the lilacs to be in bloom and too early for the roses or for honeysuckle. "What a mess," he finally said.

She nodded. "I can't believe how guilty I feel." She shifted positions and again the light floral scent teased his senses.

He suddenly realized the pleasant fragrance was coming from her. He frowned thoughtfully. Had she always smelled so good? He couldn't remember ever paying much attention before, and for some reason he found it vaguely disturbing.

He stood and walked over to the porch railing and stared out into the night. "I think your mother and mine have developed an instant case of wedding fever," he said.

He heard her rise from the swing and a moment later she stood next to him, also peering out into the distance. "I think my mother had already written me off as a hopeless case. She figured I was going to be an old maid all my life."

"That's ridiculous. You're not even thirty yet. Lots of women wait and marry in their thirties."

She smiled up at him. "Not in this town. In Foxrun little girls are raised to covet two things…the Miss Dairy Cow crown and a wedding ring."

He knew she was right. The small town had old-fashioned values when it came to their womenfolk. "How come you never entered the Miss Dairy Cow contest?" he asked curiously.

Her green eyes glowed in the light that shone from the front windows. "Be serious, Bailey," she scoffed. "I knew at a very early age my limitations. A skinny, freckle-faced girl with red hair isn't exactly beauty queen material."

Before he could reply the front door flew open. "Here they are," his mother exclaimed. "Come on, you two. We were all wondering where you disappeared. Get back in here to your party. I've got a little presentation for you."

Bailey and Mellie exchanged wary glances as they went back into the house.

"Attention…attention everyone." Luella banged on the table with her hand.

"For goodness sake, Lu, you're shaking the whole table," Henry exclaimed.

Bailey winced, wishing just once his parents

wouldn't snipe at one another. He'd had a lifetime of their bickering and had often wondered why they had remained together.

Their relationship was a large part of why he hadn't figured on marrying. He'd put aside his reservations about marriage when he'd met the lovely Stephanie, but she'd managed to destroy whatever illusions of love and happiness he'd momentarily believed in.

He'd learned everything he needed to know about marital bliss through his parents, then with his marriage to Stephanie. As far as he was concerned, a marriage certificate was nothing more than a binding contract to allow two people to bicker and moan at each other for the rest of their lives.

"Henry, hand me my purse," Luella said, bringing Bailey back to the moment at hand.

Bailey's father did as she bade, giving her the large black purse the size of a small suitcase. Mellie stood beside him and cast him a glance of curiosity. He shrugged, indicating to her he had no idea what his mother was doing.

She withdrew a small box. "Bailey and Melanie, this is the ring Henry gave me years ago when he was courting me and asked for my hand in marriage." She flipped open the jewelry box lid to reveal a delicate gold ring fashioned in a heart shape with a ruby in the center.

She walked over to where Bailey and Mellie stood and pulled the ring from its resting place. "I know it isn't a diamond," she said. "Henry couldn't afford a diamond until after we'd been married for ten years."

"Had to work overtime for years to buy a big diamond and shut her up," Henry quipped. The crowd responded with laughter.

"Anyway," Luella continued, nonplussed, "this ring has lots of sentimental value to me. I didn't give it to Bailey for that woman he brought home from college, but nothing would please me more than to see this ring on Melanie's finger."

She pushed the ring into Bailey's hand, and reluctantly he took it, aware of everyone watching. "Thanks, Mom." He leaned forward and kissed Luella's cheek.

"Well, don't just stand there, put it on Melanie's finger," Luella exclaimed. "I see that even though the two of you are engaged, her finger is quite bare."

Bailey turned to Mellie, whose eyes were as wide as he'd ever seen them. He knew exactly what she was thinking. It was the same thing he was thinking. Somehow, some way, they had both gotten in over their heads.

He took her left hand in his, for the first time noticing how small her hand was and that her nails were painted a pearly pink. Her hand was also ice-cold and trembling slightly. He slid the ring on her finger, then instantly dropped her hand.

"Kiss her," somebody from the crowd yelled, and the others took up the cry.

"Kiss her!"

"Kiss her!"

Bailey felt his face warm and he looked at her and noted that her cheeks were pink as well. He leaned down and kissed her as he had a thousand times before, a light peck on the lips.

Instantly they were met with boos.

"I kiss my grandma better than that," a male voice shouted derisively.

"Come on, Bailey boy, lay one on her," another voice exclaimed.

Mellie's cheeks grew redder, and Bailey decided the best way to handle things was with a sense of humor. Dancing his eyebrows up and down in Groucho Marx fashion, he grabbed Mellie and bent her backward in his arms. As the group hooted and hollered their encouragement, he covered her mouth with his.

Shock riveted through him as he realized her lips were slightly parted, as if awaiting a lover's kiss. An act, he told himself as she wound her slender arms around his neck. She was simply playing for the crowd.

The shock of finding her mouth open beneath his was nothing compared to the electric shock of pure pleasure that coursed through him as he tasted the hot sweetness of her.

He ended the kiss quickly and stepped back from her as the crowd of people cheered their approval.

Keeping his gaze averted from her, he bowed dramatically, then sighed in relief as people went back to cake eating and chatting in small groups.

For the remainder of the party, Bailey spent the time telling himself that kissing Mellie hadn't been as pleasurable as he'd thought at the time it had happened. It had simply been the adrenaline of the moment, knowing that everyone was watching, that had made her lips feel so soft and sweet.

There was nobody happier than Bailey when the party started to break up. He stood with Mellie on the front porch, telling people goodbye and thanking them for coming.

When the last of the guests had left, leaving only him and Mellie and their parents, they all returned inside to deal with the cleanup.

As he went around the living room picking up empty glasses and paper plates, he tried to ignore the sound of his parents arguing about whether mustard potato salad was better than mayo potato salad.

He looked over to where Mellie was scrubbing down the coffee table where punch had been spilled. ''I swear, I think the two of them look for things to argue about.''

She smiled and set the floral centerpiece back in the middle of the coffee table. ''They've always done that, Bailey.''

''I know. But, sometimes it irks me more than others.'' He dumped a plate into the trash bag, then looked around to see if he'd missed any. "It looks like we've got the worst of it. You ready for me to take you home?"

"You go ahead. Mom said she'd take me home later."

Bailey nodded. "I'll just go into the kitchen and tell everyone goodbye." As he left the living room, he acknowledged to himself that since the kiss they had shared, there'd been an awkwardness between Mellie and him that worried Bailey.

She'd been unusually quiet for the remainder of the party and had rarely met his gaze. The absolute last thing he wanted to have happen was for this crazy scheme to mess things up between them. Mellie had always been the constant in his life, the one person he could talk to, depend on and have fun with without any complications.

She walked out with him to his truck, and again he was struck by the sweet floral scent that emanated from her. Why hadn't he ever noticed it before? Maybe she'd changed perfumes recently, he told himself.

Again he felt an unusual awkwardness rising between them, and he wondered what on earth was causing it. Surely it couldn't be the kiss. The kiss had meant nothing, had merely been for show.

"I'll make sure your mother gets her ring back when this is all over," she said as they reached his truck. "And if we get any wedding presents, we'll just keep them in boxes and return them to people after the divorce.''

Bailey raked a hand through his hair, regret weighing heavily in his heart. ''I think it would have been easier if I'd just told SueEllen Trexlor that I was gay.''

Mellie giggled. ''Now that would have really kept the gossipmongers happy.'' She sobered. ''I know you'd like to back out of this right now, but please don't, Bailey.'' She placed a hand on his arm and looked up at him with her big, luminous eyes.

''At one time or another I've dated practically every eligible man in this town, and I haven't connected with any of them. Give me a baby, Bailey, and I'll never ask you for another thing for the rest of our lives.''

He wanted to back out of the whole deal, knew they had probably fallen in way over their heads. But he couldn't forget how supportive Mellie had always been. After his divorce from Stephanie, she'd never asked questions, had never pried into that area of his life, but she'd been there to pick up the pieces and make him strong again.

The bottom line was that he'd never been able to tell Mellie no. And this time was no different. ''And you'll pick up my dirty socks for the duration of our marriage.''

She grinned. ''Deal.'' She held up two crossed fingers. ''Friends.''

He held up two crossed fingers. "Pals."

They met fists in a gentle bump. "Buddies," they said simultaneously.

It was a ritual born in the fourth grade when they'd had their one and only fight, and the performing of the ritual comforted Bailey.

He leaned down and kissed her cheek, then opened his truck door. "Call me tomorrow?"

"As soon as I wake up."

He got into the truck, relief flooding through him. Whatever tension he'd thought he'd felt between them earlier was gone, and they were back on old, familiar footing. She was right. They could do this and nothing would change between them.

Chapter Four

She had known since the eighth grade that Bailey had the reputation of being a great kisser. At a slumber party a poll had been taken, and Bailey had won the honor of best kisser, hands down.

Melanie hadn't been able to vote that night so long ago at the slumber party because she'd never kissed Bailey...at least not in the way the girls were talking about kissing.

Now she could vote, and she would definitely vote for Bailey as the best kisser she'd ever kissed. His lips had been soft but firm and sizzling with heat that had flooded through her from head to toe.

The kiss had been in her thoughts the moment she'd opened her eyes that morning and was still in her head as she drove to Bailey's with a carload of some of her personal items.

It was another gorgeous late-spring day filled with warmth that promised the imminent arrival of summer. She drove with the window down, enjoying the scent of the fields and pastures she passed along the way.

As she thought of the week ahead, her heart stepped up its rhythm a bit. Friday was the last day of the school year and Saturday she would marry Bailey.

Marry Bailey. It wasn't the actual marrying Bailey that caused her heart to flutter. It was what would come after the wedding ceremony. She and Bailey would have sex. And since the whole point of the marriage as far as she was concerned was to get pregnant, then it was possible they'd have sex more than once.

If his kiss had been any indication, having sex with Bailey would be magnificent...as a woman's first time should be.

As she turned up the lane and Bailey's place came into view, she consciously shoved thoughts of kissing and sex out of her mind.

She'd always loved Bailey's place. The white ranch was nestled amid towering ancient oak trees that cooled the long front porch in the summer. The porch positively begged for a swing, but Bailey refused to consider it, telling her that swings were for old married couples, not a bachelor.

She pulled up in front of the house, but not before she saw Bailey coming to greet her from the barn.

She shut off her engine and got out of the car, noting that even though it was before noon, Bailey already looked exhausted.

"Hey," he greeted her.

"Hey, yourself," she replied. "You look beat."

He raked a hand through his hair and released a deep sigh. "I got an early-morning call from the sheriff. He busted a puppy mill and needs a place to bring about twenty malnourished, dehydrated, flea-and-worm-infested dogs. I've spent most of the morning checking my medical supplies and feed to be certain I can handle them. Now I need to get the cages ready."

"Need some help?" She gestured to her car. "I can unload this stuff later."

He offered her his first smile. "That would be terrific."

"Who was operating a puppy mill?" she asked as they walked toward the barn.

"I don't know the man. He lives in the old Ellsbury place off K Highway." They reached the door, and he opened it to allow her entry.

"Barn" was too simple a word for the state-of-the-art animal hospital Bailey had created in the structure. Heated in the winter, air-conditioned in the summer, the clinic sported an examining room, an up-to-date operating room and a room just for bathing a variety of critters.

He led her through the front area and to the back of the barn, where cages lined the walls and there was a large enclosed pen for running and playing. "I need to spread some fresh straw in the pen," he said, then pointed to the cages. "They all need to be wiped down with antibacterial soap and water. There's a pail all ready there. I can't tell you how much I appreciate your help."

She smiled. "No problem. That's what friends are for."

She settled onto the floor before the cages and pulled the bucket next to her. Within minutes the barn smelled of sweet fresh straw and the tangy scent of the antibacterial soap.

"What kind of puppies?" she asked as she worked on the first cage.

"Mostly miniature schnauzers and a litter or two of cocker spaniels. The sheriff said conditions out there were absolutely deplorable."

"Poor babies," Melanie said as she moved to the second cage.

For a few minutes they worked in relative silence, the only sound that of Bailey humming beneath his breath. Bailey always hummed when he was deep in thought. It was a habit that had often gotten him in trouble with his teachers in school but was as familiar to Melanie as her own heartbeat. More often than not she found herself humming along with him.

She wondered if maybe Stephanie had found the habit irritating and that was part of the reason she'd left him. Bailey had never been real specific about what exactly had gone wrong in his marriage, only mentioning that small-town life hadn't agreed with his beautiful wife.

He finished spreading the straw and joined her at the cages, working next to her as he hummed a Beatles tune.

"Did Sheriff Bodock say when he's bringing the puppies?" she asked, noting the clean scent of him as his broad shoulder brushed hers.

"I'm expecting him anytime now. He had to figure out a way to transport the dogs and when he called, there was still a lot to sort."

"Bailey, how are you going to handle twenty puppies?"

He sat back on his haunches and frowned. "I've got the space and I've got the supplies, but I'm probably going to have to hire some part-time help."

"Like who?" she asked curiously.

"I'll probably give Susie Sinclair a call later and see if she could help me out a few hours in the morning and a few in the afternoon. She helped me out last summer and I know she's only working part-time right now at the family store."

"She's also a candidate for Miss Dairy Cow," Melanie replied, then grinned. "She would probably think it was udderly wonderful to work for the judge."

Bailey groaned. "That was really bad," he exclaimed.

She laughed. "It was, wasn't it," she agreed.

The sound of a truck rumbled in the air, and above

the engine noise rose the yipping and crying of dogs. "It would seem that our guests have arrived," Bailey said, rising to his feet.

He held out a hand to help her up off the floor. The minute his hand touched hers, she felt a sparkle of electricity travel through her fingertips into the center of her stomach. The sensation caught her by surprise, but thankfully he didn't seem to notice anything amiss.

As they walked out of the barn and into the warm sunshine, there was little time to think about what might have caused the unusual reaction to Bailey's casual touch.

Outside of the barn, chaos reigned. Not only was there a large cattle truck parked in front of the barn, but also the sheriff's car and several fire department volunteers.

"Bailey...Melanie," Sheriff Bodock greeted them with a tired smile. "I hear congratulations are in order." He looked at Melanie. "It's about time you make an honest man of him."

"I can make him a married man, but I'm not sure I can make him an honest man," she replied and earned a teasing nudge in the ribs from Bailey.

"Let's get these puppies unloaded," Sheriff Bodock said. "I brought some volunteers to help make this go as smoothly and quickly as possible. George Clairborn needs his cattle truck back in an hour."

"We'll unload them into a pen in the back of the barn for now," Bailey said.

For the next hour they all worked together to get the puppies and their mothers out of the truck and into the pen Bailey had prepared earlier. The sheriff explained to them that they hadn't been able to find the male dogs and he suspected the owner of the place had kept them at another location.

As the volunteers walked to their cars, Melanie and Bailey walked with them. Just before the driver of the cattle truck got into the driver's seat, Melanie thought she heard a faint whimper come from the back of the truck.

"Wait a minute," she said to the driver, then crawled up in the straw-strewn back and listened carefully.

"What's wrong?" Bailey peered in after her.

"I think we missed one." As the tiny sound came again, Melanie followed it to the farthest corner, where a little jet-black schnauzer was curled up, chocolate-brown eyes weeping tears.

"Hey squirt," she said and picked the little guy up in her arms. He curled against her, as if seeking not only the warmth of her chest, but also the reassuring beat of her heart, and in that instant Melanie lost her heart.

Bailey helped her down from the back end of the truck and grinned. "I know that look. Puppies always make women get that silly, dopey look in their eyes."

"You're just jealous because nobody looks at you with that silly, dopey look," she exclaimed, and hugged the little body closer against her.

He rolled his eyes, then waved to the sheriff and the volunteers as they pulled away from the barn. "My work is just beginning," he said. "These dogs need exams, medication and food and water immediately."

"Then we'd better get started," she said.

He looked at her in surprise. "You sticking around to help?"

"Sure. As your intended wife isn't my place to help my intended husband?" Funny...she said the words lightly, but they caused a fluttering heat to course through her.

"That's right. As my intended wife you're supposed to support me in my work, cook my meals and pick up my dirty socks."

She laughed, relieved that he had taken her words as lightly as she'd meant them. "I thought I told you, picking up dirty socks is out of the question," she exclaimed as they went back into the barn.

For the next three hours they bathed dirty, frightened dogs. While Bailey did the exams on each one, Melanie fed information about their physical description and condition into the computer. She also named each puppy and put each one into a cage labeled with his or her new name.

She couldn't help but admire Bailey's gentleness as he handled each one. His deep voice was soft, soothing as he ran his hands across their little bodies and looked into mouths and ears.

She wondered if he'd use that same soft, deep voice

to whisper in her ear during foreplay. The thought caused a shiver to work up her spine. Then she wondered if they would even indulge in foreplay. After all, foreplay wasn't necessary to make a baby.

Finally they were working on the last dog, the little black schnauzer she'd found hidden in the back of the truck. "He's the only black one in the bunch," Bailey observed as he examined the pooch. "And none of the adult females wanted anything to do with him."

"Poor little thing," Melanie murmured, and stroked the fur that since his bath was smooth and silky. "I'll be his mommy." She looked at Bailey curiously. "How come you don't have a dog of your own? As much as you love them, I'd think you would have half a dozen."

He shrugged and finished the exam on the puppy, then handed him to her. "I had a dog once... remember Champ?"

"Oh, yeah, I'd forgotten. But that was years ago." Champ had been a golden retriever his parents had owned for years. The dog had been hit by a car when Bailey was twelve.

Melanie remembered that day very well. Bailey had come to her house and told her Champ was dead. They had sat side by side on Melanie's parents' front porch for about an hour. Bailey hadn't cried, nor had he spoken of the deep pain that had filled his eyes.

Through the years of their friendship, Melanie had learned that Bailey shared his laughter with anyone near, shared his dreams with her, but he shared his grief with nobody.

It was dusk when they finally left the barn and headed for the house. They were both filthy and starving. But Bailey had promised her a shower and a hot meal before she left for the night.

"You know, I've been thinking," she began.

"Wow, raise the flag, shoot some fireworks, it's a moment of celebration," he teased, then laughed as she swatted him in the arm.

"I'm serious. I've been thinking about you hiring some help." They stopped at her car, where she popped open the trunk to reveal several boxes of clothing and other items.

"And what thoughts have you had on the subject?" He grabbed one of the larger boxes as she picked up another smaller one.

"I just have this week left of school, then I'll be here full-time. For this week I could come over for an hour or so each morning, then come back right after school to help. There's really no point in you hiring anyone as long as you can get through this week."

"I think that will work," he agreed as he nudged open the front door with his elbow. "Are you sure you don't mind doing that?"

"I've got to take care of my baby," she said. She dropped her box to the floor in the sparsely decorated living room.

"Thanks, I like to be taken care of." He set his

box down and grinned at her, that slightly lopsided grin that flashed his single dimple.

"I wasn't talking about you," she scoffed teasingly. "I was talking about little Squirt."

He sighed. "I suppose it won't be long and you'll want that little mutt in the house."

She danced over to where he stood. "Really, Bailey? You wouldn't mind?"

"The sheriff told me to go ahead and try to find them all good homes, and I know you've always wanted a dog."

"I have...I do, and I think he already loves me just a little bit." With exuberant excitement, she threw her arms around his neck and kissed him soundly on the cheek.

His hand automatically went to the small of her back, the casual touch shooting a fluttering heat through her. She quickly stepped away from him, disconcerted by the unexpected physical reaction to him.

"I get first dibs on the shower," she said, quickly opening the smaller of the boxes and grabbing a clean pair of shorts and a T-shirt.

"While you're doing that, I'll take care of dinner," he said as she headed down the hallway toward the bathroom.

Moments later, standing beneath a hot spray of water, she tried to dismiss her sudden sensitivity to Bailey. She supposed it was only natural that she was seeing him in a different light, given that in seven days they would be married.

It was only natural that she'd notice things about him she hadn't noticed before...like the fact that his hands were nicely shaped with long, strong fingers, like the fact that his cheek had been warm and slightly rough with faint whiskers when she'd kissed him moments before.

She finished her shower and dried and dressed quickly, then returned to the living room where Bailey was seated on the sofa sipping on a cold beer.

"I thought you were taking care of supper."

"I did. I ordered pizza, and for dessert we have Mrs. Caldwell's famous cherry pie."

"Why did she make you a pie?"

Bailey held out his beer to her. She took two sips, then returned it to him. She never drank a full beer, so long ago they'd gotten into the habit of her sipping from his.

"I'd like to think she baked me a pie just because I'm a nice guy, but when she dropped it off, she mentioned that her granddaughter, Katy Lynn, is a contestant." He stood and finished the last of his beer. "Pizza money is on the table in case it comes while I'm in the shower."

She watched as he walked away from her, her gaze taking in the width of his back, the leanness of his waist and hips. Again a swirl of heat swept through her, and she quickly averted her eyes from him and went into the kitchen to set the table for their meal.

While she loved Bailey's house on the outside, it was a typical bachelor pad on the inside. Although bright-yellow curtains hung at the kitchen window, there were no place mats or tablecloth, no canisters or centerpiece to add any additional color. The white countertop boasted only a black microwave and a can of coffee he'd forgotten to put away that morning.

When she'd packed some of her things earlier in the day, she'd been aware of a lack of warmth in Bailey's house and had added some of her own items to spiff up his place.

If she was going to live here for a month or two, she intended to make it comfortable and homey for herself. She decided not to pull out the place mats she'd packed in the bottom of one of her boxes. Once the wedding was over, she could unload her items and introduce them into the sterility of Bailey's decor.

As she set the table, she tried to dismiss the unusual feelings Bailey had evoked in her since he'd agreed to marry her. She supposed it was only natural that she'd be eyeing him as a man, rather than as her best friend. But, it was making her darned uncomfortable.

Once they made love, all this awkwardness and overawareness of him that she suddenly felt would be gone, she assured herself.

It wasn't Bailey that was making her so tense. Nor was it the thought of making love to him. It was the thought of making love with anyone that had her nervous and uptight.

In all the years Bailey had been her friend, she'd only withheld one little secret from him...the fact that she was still a virgin.

She knew that he believed she'd made love to a guy she'd dated in college, and while she'd never outright lied to Bailey, she had done nothing to make him believe anything different.

It somehow seemed right that she was giving up her virginity to the one man she trusted above all others in the world.

The doorbell rang, pulling her from her thoughts. She grabbed the money off the table and hurried to the door, where a young kid gave her the pizza Bailey had ordered.

She'd just set the pizza on the table when Bailey reappeared, clad in a clean pair of worn jeans and a white T-shirt. "Perfect timing," she exclaimed.

"Good. I'm starving." He sat across from her at the table, and they each grabbed a piece of the hot, spicy pie.

They each ate two pieces in no time flat, without conversation to interfere with the basic task of quieting hunger pangs. As Bailey reached for a third piece, Melanie shoved her plate away and leaned back in her chair.

"I guess I'd better warn you, when I left the house this morning my mother was on the phone with your mother and I don't think they were exchanging favorite recipes."

Bailey grimaced slightly. "Yeah, Mom called me practically before dawn to see if I knew what kind of flowers you'd want for the wedding ceremony."

"What did you tell her?"

"First I reminded her that we didn't want a big deal of a wedding, then I told her daisies." He flashed her a grin. "Did you think I didn't know what your favorite flower is?"

She returned his smile, once again feeling the ease of their knowledge of each other, the warm familiar camaraderie that had existed between them since the second grade. "I wasn't sure if you remembered or not."

She leaned forward and plucked a slice of pepperoni off a piece of the pie. "I know I have an irritating tendency to ramble sometimes, and I never know if you tune me out or not."

"I'm sorry, what were you saying?" He laughed as she threatened to throw the pepperoni at him. "At least we have an excuse for why we aren't going on a traditional honeymoon," he said.

"The puppies."

He nodded. "Are you sure you don't mind working with me to care for them?"

"Not at all. You finished or are you going to make a total pig of yourself?"

He waved a hand to dismiss the last of the pizza. "I'm done."

She got up and carried the leftover to the countertop where she covered it with plastic wrap, then stuck it into the refrigerator. When she turned to face him once again, his expression was somber...thoughtful. "What?" she asked, knowing he had something on his mind.

"She didn't like animals," he said.

"Who? Stephanie?" Melanie returned to the chair opposite him, surprised that he'd brought her up. He almost never talked about her.

He nodded. "She thought dogs were dirty and cats were hairy and forget about anything remotely resembling a rodent."

"Why would a woman who hates animals marry a vet?" Melanie asked.

Bailey leaned back in his chair and rubbed his chin thoughtfully. His intense blue eyes were inscrutable. "She thought she could talk me into becoming a people doctor and that we'd move to the city and live a life of wealthy prominence."

"Didn't she realize you live a life of wealthy prominence right here in Foxrun? I mean, not only are you well respected, but you even have your very own swimming hole down in the pasture."

Bailey laughed and reached across the table to grasp her hand. "Sometimes I wonder what on earth I'd do without you in my life, Mellie."

For just a moment his words created a dizzying emotion inside her. "You're the best buddy a guy could ever want," he added, effectively dispelling whatever emotion it had been that had tried to take possession of her.

She squeezed his hand, then released it and stood. "Well, of course I am," she said briskly. "And now this buddy is calling it a night and heading home."

He got up from the table and walked her to the

door. "I'll be here early in the morning. I'll bring a few more boxes and help you with the dogs."

"I'll have the coffee on." He leaned forward and gave her a perfunctory kiss on the forehead. "'Night Mellie."

"Good night, Bailey."

Moments later as she drove home, Melanie thought about what Bailey had said just before she'd left. He'd wondered what on earth he'd do without her in his life. For just a moment she'd wished he'd been talking about her as a woman, not as a friend.

She shook her head ruefully, wondering if somehow she'd been bitten by the Miss Dairy Cow crazies that seemed to have gripped the entire town.

Chapter Five

"Colette, that was absolutely wonderful," Bailey exclaimed as he shoved his empty dinner plate aside. He grinned at Tanner Rothman who sat opposite him at the table. "Tanner, you lucky old coot. Not only is she pretty, but she can cook, too."

"And in the next couple of weeks, she will once again be a successful business woman," Tanner replied, his gaze lingering on his pretty blond bride of three weeks.

"That's right." Bailey looked back at Colette. "When is your store set to open?"

"A week from tomorrow," she replied. "I'm just waiting on delivery of a bit more inventory before officially opening the doors."

"Wow, that was fast," Bailey exclaimed.

"The old feed store was in excellent shape when

we took it over and I hired a crew to work pretty much around the clock. It didn't take long to transform it into Colette's shop,'' Tanner explained.

"It's a baby shop, right?'' Bailey asked.

Colette nodded. "I carry everything a baby needs for the first four years of life.''

"Is Melanie…'' Tanner paused delicately.

"No, no,'' Bailey hurriedly replied. "She isn't pregnant right now, although she wants a baby as soon as possible.''

"Then I hope you two will be a couple of my best customers,'' Colette replied.

"Is Gina still managing your store in Kansas City?'' Gina was Tanner's younger sister.

"Yes, and doing a wonderful job despite the worries of her big brother.'' Colette reached over and lightly touched the back of Tanner's hand in a loving gesture, then stood. "And now I'll leave you two alone to man talk.'' With a lingering smile of love for her husband, she left the dining room and disappeared into the kitchen.

"So, tomorrow is the big day,'' Tanner said.

"Yeah.'' Bailey wrapped his hands around his coffee mug.

"If you'd given everyone a little more notice, I'd have arranged a bachelor party.''

"I didn't want one,'' Bailey replied. It was bad enough that Mellie's friends and family had thrown her a shower this evening. He took a sip of his coffee, fighting the urge to come clean to Tanner, to tell him that their marriage wouldn't be a real one, that it was only temporary.

"Mellie and I wanted just a simply ceremony without any fuss or bother. Unfortunately, our families had other ideas," he continued. The wedding was now to take place at the Baptist Church, with a huge reception to follow at the community center.

"I'll tell you one thing, Bailey. There's nothing quite like marriage, nothing like exploring the secrets of the woman you love."

"Mellie doesn't have any secrets from me. Sometimes I think I know her better than I know myself," Bailey replied.

Tanner laughed as if enjoying his own private joke. "You're in for a rude awakening, Bailey. Women have more secrets than old barn cats have fleas, and discovering them only intensifies the intimacy of the marriage."

Tanner laughed once again and reared back in his chair. "Listen to me, I sound like some sort of advertisement for the sensitive male of the century." He leaned forward. "But honestly, Bailey, I've never been as happy as I am with Colette."

Bailey saw the happiness on Tanner's face. It curved his friend's mouth, shone from his eyes and for just a moment a shaft of envy swept through Bailey.

He shoved the uncomfortable feeling away as he stood. "I hate to eat and run, but I do have a big day tomorrow." The big slice of pot roast he'd just eaten sat heavily in his stomach as he thought of the wedding the next day.

Tanner rose as well. "I'll walk you out."

"Tell Colette thanks for the wonderful meal," Bailey said as the two men stepped outside onto Tanner's porch.

"No problem," Tanner replied. "I hear the town council appointed you as the judge for the Miss Dairy Cow Contest."

"Yeah. Why did you back out?"

Tanner shrugged his broad shoulders. "The main reason was because I'd promised Colette the minute she moved here from Kansas City, we'd get her shop up and running. I wasn't sure how much time that was going to require. So, have you seen SueEllen Trexlor naked yet?"

Bailey shot a startled look at Tanner, who laughed. "How did you know?"

"Right before I withdrew my name as judge SueEllen showed up here one night wearing a raincoat and nothing else."

"She was in my shower the other day, waiting to help scrub my back," Bailey explained.

"Poor SueEllen." Tanner shook his head ruefully. "She wants that crown badly and doesn't realize displaying herself won't get it for her." Tanner grinned. "But she does have a nice figure, doesn't she?"

Bailey returned the grin. "I didn't notice."

"Yeah, right," Tanner replied dryly as Bailey got

into his truck. "We'll see you tomorrow evening at the reception."

Tomorrow evening at the reception. Tanner's words echoed inside Bailey's head as he drove home. More than once that day he'd had to fight the desire to phone Mellie and call the whole thing off.

He'd definitely overreacted to the whole Miss Dairy Cow thing, had been vulnerable because of SueEllen's naked appearance and had fallen prey to Mellie's crazy scheme for a baby.

Still, even though he'd wanted to call her and back out, he hadn't. It was no longer a matter of just letting Mellie down.

Things had spiraled way out of control. In the past week his mother and Mellie's mother had been like twin tornadoes, blowing away any obstacles that stood in the way of a day to remember.

Flowers had been ordered, a caterer found, the community center had been reserved and a band had been hired. He'd been fitted for a black tux with yellow cummerbund and tie, and wedding gifts had been arriving at the house for the past three days.

He had a feeling nothing short of his death could force an end to the events he and Mellie had set into motion.

One thing easy to dismiss was Tanner's assertion that part of a marriage was discovering each other's secrets. Mellie with her bright-green eyes and freckled face was like an open book to him.

He knew what she liked to eat and how her nose

turned bright red when she cried. He knew her politics tended to lean to the right, that her left-front tooth was a crown and that her nickname when growing up had been "skinny, minny Melanie."

He certainly had no secrets from Mellie and he hadn't been lying when he'd told Tanner that he knew her better than he knew himself.

No, there would be no surprises, no wondrous awakenings to deepen any marital intimacy between Mellie and him. Hopefully he could succeed in getting her pregnant right away, then they could have a quiet separation and an uncomplicated divorce.

But what about the baby? A little voice whispered in his head. For the first time he considered the outcome of this deal with Mellie. The outcome would be a tiny human being...Bailey's baby.

Bailey had never thought much about having children. Stephanie had made it clear when they'd married that she wasn't particularly interested in having a family. Bailey had suspected she felt the same way about children that she did about animals...they were messy and dirty and required too much attention.

He parked his car in front of his house, then walked to the barn to check on the pups. No wonder he loved dogs. They were so remarkably uncomplicated. Feed them, water them and scratch them behind the ears, and they offered back unconditional love.

He only hoped this brief marriage to Mellie remained as uncomplicated as it had sounded when they'd first agreed to it.

*   *   *

Melanie stood before the mirror in the church's ladies' room, staring at the reflection of the bride in the glass. She'd told her mother all week she didn't want a wedding dress, that her beige suit would work just fine, but Marybeth Watters was not about to allow her daughter to be married in an old suit.

The dress they'd finally agreed upon was a simple, but traditional white gown. A slick silk with tiny seed buttons down the front, it clung to Melanie like a second skin, delicately displaying the thrust of her breasts and the slenderness of her waist.

Her hair had been braided and coiled around her head, the bright copper color broken up by baby's breath and daisies tucked into the coils.

"You look beautiful," her mother said, and turned her around to face her.

Melanie wrinkled up her nose with a rueful grin. "I look as beautiful as a freckle-faced, redheaded woman can look."

"Nonsense," Marybeth said. "You look absolutely beautiful." With tears sparkling in her eyes, she hugged Melanie. "I'm so happy for you, dear. I just know you and Bailey are going to be so happy together. The whole town has known for years that the two of you were meant for each other. We've just been waiting for the two of you to realize it."

Guilt swept through Melanie as she returned her mother's hug. She swore that once this particular lie was finished and over, she'd never do anything like this again. In the end her mother would forgive her the broken marriage if Melanie presented her with a new grandbaby.

"I'm going to check to see that everything is ready. I'll be right back, dear." As her mother left the small room, Melanie turned back to face the mirror.

There was nothing Marybeth Watters loved more dearly than her grandchildren. Her bout with cancer a year before had made Melanie realize how short life could be and had driven into a frenzy Melanie's desire to have a child.

And now it was finally going to happen. Her cheeks pinkened as she thought of the night to come. She moved away from the mirror and to the window, where dusk was cascading with purple hues to claim the last of the day's light.

In just a few minutes she and Bailey would be married, and tonight, after the reception, they would go to his house and she would crawl into his bed. They would have sex and hopefully make a baby.

Before the shiver that had started at the base of her spine worked its way fully to her shoulders, her mother opened the door. Eyes shining with the tears Melanie knew she would shed during the brief ceremony, she simply said, "It's time."

Melanie picked up her bouquet from the counter and drew a deep, steadying breath. She didn't know why she suddenly felt so nervous.

It was Bailey, for crying out loud. Bailey, who had reluctantly dressed up like a sheep to play opposite her Bo Peep one Halloween, Bailey, who had taken her on her first roller coaster ride. He was her very best friend. As quickly as the nerves had stretched taut inside her, they relaxed. It was just good old Bailey, and everything was going to be fine.

As Melanie stepped out of the rest room and into the hallway, she heard the swell of the organ music playing the bridal march.

The group inside the sanctuary would be small. Both Melanie and Bailey had insisted that only immediate family members be allowed into the church. However, Melanie suspected most of the entire town would turn out for the reception following the ceremony.

Her father awaited her, and with a gentle smile he took her arm in his. "You look gorgeous, pumpkin," he said softly.

"Thanks, Dad." She squeezed his arm tightly and then the two of them began the slow walk up the center aisle of the church.

Her heart pounded in her ears, and nervous tension made her feel a slightly suffocating sensation. Then she saw Bailey. He stood next to the preacher, tall and handsome in the black tux. His yellow bow tie was slightly crooked, and he had a look of sheer panic on his face as his gaze darted around the room as though seeking a quick exit.

Then he saw her and his eyes widened slightly as if in surprise. Melanie fought against an impulse to giggle. She couldn't believe they were actually doing this and knew he was feeling the same sort of surreal disbelief that she was.

As her father gave her hand to Bailey, she winked at him. One corner of his lips curved up in a half smile and he winked back. Within five minutes they were officially man and wife.

The kiss that sealed their union was the kind Melanie was accustomed to receiving from Bailey, a light sweet peck on the lips.

"I can't believe we did this," he said a few minutes later when they were in his truck and headed toward the community center. He pulled at his tie, as if it was in the process of slowly strangulating him. "By the way, you don't look bad in a wedding dress."

"Thanks, and you aren't totally ugly in a tux," she replied, returning his backhanded compliment.

He flashed her a quick grin as he pulled into the already crowded parking area of the community center. He found a parking place, pulled in, then cut the engine and turned to her. "Well, we did it."

"We did half of it," she replied and to her surprise felt the warmth of a blush stealing over her cheeks. "I have now officially saved you from the claws of the crown-crazed single women of Foxrun. Now all you have to do is fulfill your end of our bargain."

"You want me to do that right here? Right now? I'll try, but I have a feeling the stick shift might get in the way."

Although he was teasing her, she saw an edge of

tension in his eyes, felt it radiating from him. Or was she feeling her own edge of tension about the night to come?

"I think before we do anything rash, we should probably go inside and enjoy the reception your mother and mine spent hours pulling together."

"You're right." He pocketed his keys and opened his door. "Time to go in and pretend to be the happily-in-love-forever couple."

It was all a game of pretend, Melanie reminded herself as she and Bailey walked toward the community center. He held her hand, his fingers strong and warm wrapped around hers.

There was a crowd of well-wishers standing just outside the door, and Melanie and Bailey's appearance was greeted with cheers as bird seed rained down on their heads.

Laughing, they raced toward the door and entered the community center, which had been transformed by their mothers into a ribbon-and-crepe-paper wonderland.

A lace-covered table at the front of the large room held a fountain spewing champagne and a three-tier wedding cake.

The band members were tuning instruments on the small bandstand in one corner, and the long banquet tables were filled with friends and neighbors and acquaintances.

Melanie lost Bailey as she was engulfed in dozens of hugs. She was passed like a football from arms to arms, hugged and kissed and congratulated until the faces began to blur in her mind.

She caught a glimpse of Bailey, being slapped on the back and kissed on the cheek by well-wishers. He had the same dazed look on his face that she knew covered her own, as well.

Her mother rescued them, grabbing first Melanie by the arm, then Bailey and leading them to a table with a beautiful centerpiece. "You two sit here," she instructed. "In just a little while the band is going to play the first dance just for the two of you."

They both sat. "I feel like I've just been mauled by a wild pack of rabid dogs," Bailey said as he straightened his tie.

Melanie laughed. "They all mean well." She frowned as she saw a familiar old man making tracks toward them, a glass of champagne in each hand. "Uh-oh, here comes my uncle Jack," she warned Bailey.

Jack Watters, while one of Melanie's favorite relatives, was also more than a little bit outspoken and eccentric. He plopped the glasses of champagne on the table before them. "Drink up," he exclaimed. "You're several glasses behind everyone else in the room."

"Thanks, Jack," Bailey said and took a sip of the bubbly.

Jack clapped Bailey on the back. "If it was a hundred years ago, we wouldn't be sitting here at this reception. We'd be throwing a jamboree, beating pots and pans outside your window while the two of you consummated your marriage. But this being the century that it is, I imagine you two have been going at it like rabbits for years.''

"Uncle Jack!" Melanie exclaimed as Bailey laughed.

"Ah, loosen up, Melanie," Uncle Jack replied, then ambled away from their table.

That's exactly what Melanie tried to do as the party wore on. She danced the obligatory first dance with Bailey, cut the cake with him and shared a toast. But with each moment that passed, rather than loosening up, she was tightening up.

Bailey on the other hand was definitely getting more and more loose as the night wore on. She'd lost count of the number of glasses of champagne he'd drunk, but the intense sparkle in his eyes and the slight flush on his cheeks let her know he was precariously close to his limit.

She, too, had drunk more champagne than usual, but each glass she drank seemed to make her more stone-cold sober. Tonight. The thought of her and Bailey in bed together caused every nerve ending in her body to tingle with a strange kind of energy, and the sensations were only getting worse with each passing minute.

She looked out onto the dance floor where Bailey was dancing with her aunt Nancy. He'd shed his tux jacket long ago, and his shirt was unbuttoned to expose a tuft of dark chest hair.

Bailey loved to dance and he did it well, moving with a natural rhythm and grace that Melanie had always envied. She had two left feet on the dance floor and considered dancing as desirous an activity as a root canal. Bailey had already danced with nearly every woman in the room, and in the past hour the crowd had begun to thin.

Melanie thought it was protocol that the bride and groom leave the reception before the bulk of the guests did. With this thought in mind, she stood with the intention of reining in her husband and taking him home.

Her husband. Bailey's mother's ring on her finger felt cold and alien, as it had from the moment he'd slipped it on her hand.

He was her temporary husband, but also her lifetime friend, she reminded herself, and this thought dispelled some of the tension she'd been feeling about the night to come.

She stood at the edge of the dance floor until the band stopped playing and Bailey and her aunt stopped dancing, then she walked over to Bailey. "I think it's time we make an exit," she said. "It's customary for the bride and groom to leave before the guests."

"It is?" He cast her a big grin. "We certainly want to be customary, don't we?" He threw an arm around her shoulder, and as they made their way toward the door, telling people thank you and goodbye, she noticed he was more than a little unsteady on his feet.

"Maybe it would be best if you drive," he said as

they approached his truck. He dug into his pocket for the car keys. "I'll be fine by the time we get to my place. I'm just feeling a little bit woozy."

"I'll be happy to drive."

Within minutes they were heading in the direction of Bailey's house. Bailey, apparently still functioning beneath the haze of an alcoholic buzz, was talkative, as she knew he tended to get when he drank.

"Did you have a good time?" he asked. "I had a great time," he replied, not waiting for her to answer. "I never knew it could be so much fun to get married. Stephanie and I didn't have a reception or anything like that. Of course, if we had, she would have been totally ticked off with me for dancing with everyone. But you aren't mad, are you?"

"No, I'm not mad," she replied, keeping her gaze focused on the road. "I know how much you love to dance."

"That's one good thing about you and me, Mellie. We understand each other." He reached over and patted her on the shoulder. "You're a champ, Mellie."

She wasn't feeling like a champ. As she parked the truck in front of Bailey's house, she felt like nothing more than a mass of bunched and bundled nerves.

For years she'd dreamed of losing her virginity on her wedding night, and always in those dreams she was giving herself to a prince of a man who loved her with a depth of emotion that was overwhelming.

Instead, she'd given up those dreams and twisted

Bailey's arm into marrying her so she could have the child her heart so desired.

They got out of the truck, and Bailey staggered slightly as he took the porch stairs. "You don't really want me to carry you over the threshold, do you?" he asked.

"I would expect and demand it if this was a real marriage," she said, although in her heart she couldn't help but think it might have been nice under different circumstances.

"You might want to check the kitchen before you come back to the bedroom," Bailey said once they were inside.

"What did you do? Leave me dirty dishes as a wedding present?" she asked.

Bailey grinned, his eyes not quite focusing on her, then he turned and stumbled down the hallway toward the bedroom.

Melanie headed into the kitchen, surprised to discover a child's gate barring the entryway. Behind the gate, bedecked with a silver bow around his neck, tail wagging at the sight of her, was Squirt.

"Oh, Bailey," she whispered as she reached over the gate and picked up the wiggly puppy. She knew the devastation of Champ's loss so long ago had kept Bailey from ever wanting a dog as a housemate again.

She also knew that he'd allowed Squirt into the house because he knew she'd always wanted a dog. Her parents had never allowed an animal in the house, and when she'd moved out into her apartment, it had a no-pet policy.

She hugged the puppy to her chest for a long moment, feeling warm and fuzzy inside. Suddenly she wasn't worried about making love with Bailey. All the tension that thoughts of this night had brought was gone beneath the warmth of Squirt against her and the wonder of Bailey's thoughtfulness.

Having sex with Bailey was going to be just fine. There was no reason for sex to ruin the magic of their friendship. She kissed Squirt and placed him back behind the gate, then headed for the bedroom.

She stopped in the doorway, all her hopes for the night seeping out of her. Bailey was diagonal across the bed, obviously passed out. His shirt was half-unbuttoned, as if he'd crashed to the bed in the middle of undressing.

She'd known he was drinking more than he was accustomed to, had known that he was slightly loopy on the drive home, but apparently she'd underestimated just how under-the-influence he'd been.

And why had he drunk so much? Bailey often enjoyed a beer in the evenings, but he almost never overindulged. Melanie swept into his bathroom and grabbed the nightclothes that were folded on a shelf in the linen closet.

Over the past week she'd moved most of her personal items here in preparation for their brief, but hopefully fruitful, marriage.

Clutching the nightclothes to her breast, she left the

master bedroom and went into one of the guest bedrooms. She was surprised by the well of emotion that
pressed against her chest as she took off the wedding
gown and slipped into the satin camisole and tap
pants.

There was no denying she was disappointed. There
would certainly be no hope for a baby with her sleeping in here and Bailey passed out in the next room.

But what surprised her was a niggling fear that
swept into her head. As she crawled beneath the blan-
kets on the bed, she found herself wondering if per-
haps the reason Bailey had drunk so much was because he simply couldn't face having sex with her.

Chapter Six

Before Bailey opened his eyes, he knew he had the hangover from hell. His head pounded with a nauseating intensity, and his mouth was achingly dry and wicked tasting.

Dear heaven, but he had tied one on the night before. He couldn't remember the last time he'd gotten that drunk. Certainly it had been years.

For long moments he remained on the bed, eyes closed, and thought of the night before. He'd done exactly what he'd feared he would do—he'd let Mellie down.

Anxiety had gripped him the moment he'd seen her walking down the church aisle toward him. He'd never seen her looking so...so amazing. Her coppery hair had shone with a breathtaking radiance, and the gown had clung to curves he had never noticed she possessed.

And that night she expected him to not only make love to her but to make a baby.

What if he couldn't? Although he'd never considered it before, what if he couldn't make a baby? That anxious thought had been followed by another. What if Mellie hated the way he made love? And for that matter should he kiss her, caress her, or would that offend her?

One worry had followed another and another, and he'd found himself drinking to alleviate his concerns. He didn't even remember how they had gotten home.

He opened his eyes and sat up, grabbing the sides of his head to keep it from rolling off his spine. Lordy, but he had a headache.

And where was Mellie? He owed her a huge apology. Gingerly he stood and walked to the bedroom doorway. From his vantage point he could see directly into the guest room across the hall. Mellie's wedding dress hung on a hanger in the opened closet, and the bed wasn't made.

So, that's where she'd spent her wedding night. He grimaced as his head banged a painful beat. He definitely owed her an apology. But first...a shower.

Moments later, standing beneath a near-scalding stream of water, Bailey began to feel more like a human being again. His head stopped pounding and he was now eager to make things right with Mellie.

He dried and dressed in a pair of jeans and a

T-shirt, then headed for the kitchen, where the scent of fresh-brewed coffee rose tantalizingly in the air.

The first perk of being married, he thought to himself. The coffee was already made.

He found Mellie seated at the kitchen table, Squirt dancing at her feet. He stepped over the gate, keeping Squirt imprisoned on the tile floor, and offered an apologetic smile to Mellie.

"Am I in the doghouse?" he asked.

"No, you're in the kitchen," she replied with a teasing smile.

Relief swept through him. Thank God Mellie wasn't the type of woman to hold a grudge. He poured himself a cup of coffee, then joined her at the table, where yellow place mats had appeared as if by magic.

"Ah, one night in my house and you're already girlifying it," he said.

"I haven't even begun. Ever since you bought this place, I've had an itching to do a little decorating." She took a sip of her coffee, her gaze meeting his over the rim of her mug. "So, how's the head this morning?"

"If you'd asked me fifteen minutes earlier, I would have told you to cut it off and put me out of my misery. But, after a hot shower, I'm actually not feeling too bad." He took a drink from his mug, giving him seconds to figure out how to best make an apology to her.

He set his mug down on the place mat, but kept

his hands wrapped around it. "Mellie...about last night. I'm sorry. I don't know what got into me."

A small smile curved her lips. "I do...about two bottles of champagne got into you."

He smiled sheepishly, then the smile fell as he saw a glimmer of pain in her eyes. "Mellie, I know you were expecting me to begin to fulfill my end of this bargain last night, and I feel awful about getting drunk and passing out."

"It's all right," she replied. She looked down into her coffee cup and continued, "Bailey, I know I'm not like the women you're used to dating. I mean, I'm not blond or stunning, and I'm not...you know, that built." She looked at him again, her cheeks more than a little bit pink. "I understand if, you know, your desire isn't really high. I just wanted you to know that maybe if we'd do it in complete darkness, then you could, like, pretend that I'm somebody else."

Bailey stared at her, stunned by her words. "Yeah, or maybe we could just put a paper bag over your head."

"If you think that would help," she replied.

He was utterly astonished. "Jeez, Mellie, I was just kidding! How shallow do you think I am?"

She shrugged, her gaze once again shooting away from his. "I just know that you tend to like the Miss Dairy Cow contestant kind of woman, and we both know that's not me."

Bailey couldn't believe what he was hearing. He'd

never before realized what a lack of confidence Mellie had in her own attractiveness.

True, nobody would ever say she was breathtakingly beautiful, or heart-stoppingly stunning, but she was certainly more than pretty. Her eyes were the color of new grass, fringed with long brownish-red lashes. Her hair was a spill of curly copper that sparked with golden lights, and her mouth was a Cupid's bow of daintiness.

As he stared at her mouth, he thought of the kiss they had shared on the night of their engagement party. He'd been shocked to find her mouth so warm, so sweet and yielding. Suddenly he wanted to kiss her again...badly.

"I suppose you think I drank too much last night so I would be able to face the prospect of making love to you."

Again she looked away from him. "The thought did enter my mind," she admitted softly.

A rush of emotion swept through him. This woman had been at his side for every important, momentous occasion of his life. Whenever he'd fallen, she'd picked him up and brushed him off, and when he'd celebrated anything, she'd always been the most fun reveler.

And she was afraid she was so unattractive he'd have to get bombed out of his head in order to make love to her.

He stood from the table and held out his hand to her. "Mellie."

She frowned, eyeing him curiously. "What?"

"Come here." He took her hand and pulled her up from her chair. Without giving her a chance to react, he instantly covered her mouth with his.

For a moment she remained stiff and unyielding in his arms, but as he touched his tongue to hers, delving into the sweetness of her mouth, some of the tenseness seemed to leave her and a different kind of tension began to fill him.

She smelled like summer flowers, and through the thin material of her cotton dress he felt the soft thrust of her breasts against his chest.

It had been a long time since Bailey had been with a woman. A year ago he'd had a brief relationship with a woman named Kathryn. The relationship had sizzled for about two weeks, then fizzled and extinguished as quickly as it had begun.

But at the moment there were no thoughts of any other women in his head. All he wanted to do for Mellie was prove to her that she was attractive and desirable.

He broke the kiss and once again took her by the hand, surprised to find hers ice-cold. "Come with me," he said.

"Where?" she asked, slightly breathless.

He smiled at her. "I think it's time I work on fulfilling my end of the bargain."

Her eyes flared wide with panic. "But, Bailey, it's daytime."

He quirked an eyebrow upward in amusement. "There's a rule about these things?"

"Well, no...but it might make it harder for you to pretend."

He touched the cheek of her so-familiar face. "Mellie, I don't have to pretend." Before she could say another word, he pulled her through the gate of the kitchen and down the hallway to his bedroom. With each step they took, her hand seemed to grow colder.

"You want to back out of our deal?" he asked softly when they stood facing each other at the foot of the bed.

"No," she replied swiftly. "Do you?"

As an answer he claimed her mouth once again, and once again he was surprised by the sweet heat of her. He'd had no idea she was so good at kissing, and he was equally surprised by his immediate physical response.

They had been kissing for long moments before her arms raised and she tentatively wound them around his neck. He had hugged Mellie a million times in the past, but now with her body so tightly against his he became aware of things he'd never noticed before.

Heat radiated from her body, and although thin, she wasn't "skinny, minny Melanie" anymore. She had curves where women were supposed to have curves.

He moved his hands up and down her back, finally coming to rest at the top of her zipper on the back of her dress. She gasped, a tiny, almost imperceptible sound.

He moved his mouth from hers, trailing kisses down the warm sweet flesh of her neck and throat. Again she gasped and he found his desire growing as he realized she found his touch, his kiss pleasurable.

Pulling the zipper down, he was shocked when she moved her hands and slid them up the back of his T-shirt. So, she wasn't just going to be a passive partner, but rather a willing participant.

His blood heated, and suddenly he forgot all the reasons why he'd once thought this would be a bad idea. He forgot that Mellie was his very best friend in the whole wide world.

All he knew was that he wanted her right here and right now. And unless she demurred, he was going to have her.

Any doubts Melanie might have entertained about this moment were swept entirely away by the passion she tasted in Bailey's kisses, the fire in his fingertips.

The clean scent of him wrapped around her, as familiar and comforting as her old flannel pajamas on a wintry night.

It surprised her somewhat, that she felt no embarrassment, no inkling of shyness. It simply felt right with him.

As he pulled her dress from her shoulders, she allowed it to fall to the floor, a puddle of coral cotton.

She stood before him clad only in a white silk demi bra and a pair of wispy white silk panties.

He stepped back from her and pulled his shirt over his head, then, eyes locked with hers, popped the button of his jeans. His eyes glittered as he lowered the zipper and pulled off the jeans, leaving him clad only in a pair of cotton briefs.

"Okay?" he asked softly.

The fact that he'd asked made her more than okay. She nodded her head, and he wrapped his arms around her and lowered her to the bed.

She'd wondered if, when they finally had sex, there would be foreplay, and now the question was answered. Bailey seemed to be in no hurry to complete the act.

As he captured her lips in another of his breathtaking kisses, his hands moved languidly up and down the bare skin of her back, as if he had all the hours in the world to explore the wonder of her skin.

By the time his fingers worked to unclasp her bra, she was ready to take the next step in their intimacy. All jittery first-time fears were gone. She knew implicitly that Bailey would be gentle and sweet and would never do anything to hurt her, either physically or emotionally.

She tried to remind herself that this had nothing to do with pleasure, but was a means to an end. A baby. That's what she wanted from Bailey and that's what this was all about. He was fulfilling his end of their bargain.

But it was difficult to focus on that aspect when pleasure soared through her at his every touch. He removed her bra and ran his hands over her breasts, causing her nipples to tauten in response.

When he captured one of her nipples in his mouth, she gasped in surprise as tingles of electricity raced through her entire body. She had never had anyone touch her with such intimacy, and once again she was grateful that it was Bailey who was introducing her into the world of sensual pleasure.

She raked her hands over his broad back, loving the feel of the play of his muscles beneath her fingertips and loving the moan that came from the back of his throat.

Sensations overwhelmed her, stealing all thought, as a deep, abiding hunger awakened inside her. When he finally touched her over the silky fabric of her panties, she didn't fight the impulse to arch up to meet him.

He stroked her gently at first, in a slow rhythm that was half maddening, and the hunger inside her became ravenous. She could think of nothing but Bailey's touch, the warmth of his body against hers, the fire he evoked in the pit of her stomach.

As he increased the rhythm of his intimate caress, a tension built inside her, a tension the likes of which she'd never known before. With each stroke of his hand, the tension grew, making her feel as if she was going to scream, shatter into pieces, melt into him and never surface again.

She reached a peak of pleasure that brought tears to her eyes, and a sweet release fluttered through her, leaving her gasping and spent.

Before she could recover, in two swift movements he'd removed her panties and his briefs. He positioned himself between her thighs and attempted to ease into her.

He stiffened, shock on his features as he was met with resistance. "Mellie?" He began to ease backward, but she grabbed his hips and pulled him back to her.

"Don't stop, Bailey," she whispered. "It's all right. It's what I want."

His gaze held hers for an aching, long moment, then he closed his eyes and took full possession of her. Melanie had expected pain, and there was some pain, but it was manageable.

For long moments he made no movement, as if afraid any further action might hurt her. But the initial pain had ebbed and her body reacted with instincts as old as time. She moved her hips, and he moaned, a deep, low sound that resonated inside her.

She could feel his heartbeat against her own, and she wasn't sure whose was racing faster. His moan seemed to break the spell of his inertia and gently he pulled back just a little, then gently thrust forward. Again he moaned, as if the sensation was too great to bear.

As he moved again, sweetly, devastatingly against

her, she felt the now-familiar rise of tension once again filling her up.

"Bailey..." She wanted the taste of his name on her lips as she rode the waves of pleasure. His skin was a golden bronze in the sunlight dancing through the window, and she remembered that day she'd seen him naked out by the pond. He looked as beautiful now as he had then.

He looked at her, his eyes glowing an intense blue, then his lips found hers and they kissed, a deep, passionate meeting of their lips that stole her breath and swept her higher into a flaming vortex of sensation.

Suddenly everything became more frenzied. He moved faster against her, and she welcomed the quickened pace. She had never known that sex could be so beautiful, so utterly awesome and wondered if it was just sex that was so good, or sex with Bailey that was so good.

She had no time to ponder the question, for all too quickly she was swept away by the new release that shuddered through her. At the same time Bailey stiffened against her and cried out her name.

For a long moment they remained unmoving, their breaths raspy and uneven in the otherwise silent room. With a suddenness that startled her, he rolled off her and stood. Instantly she grabbed for the sheet to cover her nakedness.

"You should have told me." His tone was razor sharp as he grabbed his briefs and pulled them on.

She didn't try to pretend she didn't know what he was talking about. "What difference does it make?"

He stepped into his jeans, a pulse ticking at his taut jaw. "Trust me, it makes a difference."

Without waiting for her reply, he grabbed his T-shirt from the floor and left the room. A moment later she heard the slam of the front door and knew he had left the house.

The warm glow that had surrounded her left, usurped by a cold chill as she realized how angry Bailey was with her. That pulse in the muscle of his jaw only ticked when he was really mad.

Reluctantly she slid out from beneath the sheet and stood. She needed to talk to him, to make things right. She'd never been able to stand it when Bailey was mad at her, and this time was no different. She dressed quickly, then headed out to the barn where she knew he would be.

Chapter Seven

Bailey placed a measurement of food into the cage that contained the puppy Mellie had named Biscuit and fought against the anger that still swept through him.

She should have told him. Dammit, she should have told him that she was a virgin. Had he known, he would never have agreed to any of this.

A woman's first time should be with a lover, not a friend. He'd just assumed she and Randy Sinclair, the young man she'd dated in college, had shared a completely intimate relationship. She'd effectively lied to him and put him in the uncomfortable position of being her first lover.

There was not supposed to have been any surprises where Mellie was concerned, but he'd just received a whopper of a surprise. That, coupled with the fact that he'd found making love to Mellie to be far more pleasurable than he'd ever dreamed had him feeling irritated and out of sorts.

He moved to the next cage, noting that the little schnauzer inside seemed rather listless. He hoped he didn't lose any more of the pups. In the past week three had been too sick for him to save.

"Bailey?"

He didn't turn at the sound of her voice, but rather continued his task of measuring dog food.

"Oh, okay, so you're in one of your 'pouty, I'm going to ignore you' moods," she said, moving close enough to him that he could smell the scent of her perfume.

"I don't have pouty moods," he replied, refusing to look at her. She laughed. He tensed. He'd never noticed before that her low, slightly throaty laughter sounded rather provocative.

"You should have told me," he repeated. He finally turned to face her. She'd apparently hurried outside. She was barefoot, her dress was unzipped and her hair was a wild cloud of burnished curls. "You owed me the truth. I would never have agreed to this if you'd told me the truth."

"Oh, honestly, Bailey." She planted her hands on her hips. "It's not like I actually lied to you."

"You told me you and Randy were intimate," he replied.

She shook her head, causing her wild curls to dance around her shoulders. "I did not. You just assumed that, because Randy and I dated for a while. Besides, what difference does it make?''

"Now it doesn't make any difference, what's done is done." He grimaced. "But if I'd known ahead of time, I never would have agreed to this."

"So you keep saying, but why?" She took another step toward him and placed a hand on his arm. Her fingers were warm, and Bailey suddenly remembered how those fingers had felt caressing his naked back. He stepped away from her touch and instead raked a hand through his hair.

"Mellie...a woman's first time is supposed to be with somebody special. They say women always remember their first lover."

"So, you're saying you aren't special and I should just forget you?"

Bailey sighed in frustration, knowing she was trying to tease him into not being upset with her. He wasn't sure why, but he felt as if she'd somehow betrayed him by not telling him.

Funny, now that he thought about it, he and Mellie had rarely talked about sex. They had shared almost every intimate thought they'd ever had with each other, except for the sex stuff.

"Bailey." Again she placed her hand on his arm, her eyes so green...so earnest as she gazed at him. "There is no special man in my life other than you, and I knew it would be all right with you.

"Besides—" she dropped her hand "—my condition as a virgin wasn't exactly easy to casually drop

into one of our conversations.'' She paused a moment. ''Here, Bailey, have another piece of pizza,
and, oh, by the way, I'm a virgin.''

He couldn't help but grin, especially since her ar-
gument so closely matched his most recent thoughts.
But his smile quickly fell and once again he raked a
hand through his hair. ''I just hope things don't get
all complicated between us,'' he finally said. ''You
know...crazy.'' He averted his gaze from hers.

He felt her gaze on him, then she laughed. ''What
are you afraid of, Bailey? That just because you've
kissed me, had sex with me, that I'll fall madly in
love with you and will beg you to stay married to
me?''

She picked up a morsel of dried dog food from the
floor and threw it at him. ''Get over yourself. I know
you too well to think you could ever be the kind of
husband I'd want.''

Before he had time to reply, the crunch of gravel
from the driveway indicated to them that somebody
had just arrived. Mellie's eyes widened frantically,
and she raced over to where Bailey stood.

''Zip me!'' she exclaimed, and turned to present
him her back.

As he moved the zipper up the back of her dress,
he couldn't help but notice the sight of her slender,
freckled back, the smooth column broken only by the
strap of her bra. For just a moment he had an impulse
to pull her up against him and stroke his hands down
her warm back.

The impulse irritated him and he quickly zipped her as she reached up and smoothed her hair in an attempt to find control amid the chaos of curls.

Before they'd completely separated from each other, his mother flew in. "Here they are, Henry," she yelled. She smiled at them. "And how are our favorite newlyweds this morning?" She walked over to Mellie and patted her cheek. "You've got that newlywed glow on your face." She walked back to the door of the barn. "Henry! I said they were in here."

Bailey winced. There were times he thought his mother was part woman, part banshee. She turned back to face him and Mellie. "We've got the truck out there loaded with your wedding presents from the reception."

She pulled several sheets of paper from her purse and held them out to Mellie. "We made a list of all the things you received and from whom so you can get thank-you notes out right away."

She handed Mellie the list as Henry walked into the barn. "Now, Bailey, you'll need to unload most of the things. I don't want your father lifting anything heavy and pulling his back out. You know what a terrible patient he makes."

"Maybe that's because you aren't exactly Nurse Nightingale," Henry replied.

"I'll get started unloading things," Bailey said, unwilling to stand around and listen to his parents snipe at each other.

"And I'll just go inside and put on a fresh pot of coffee," Mellie replied.

"Coffee would be delightful," Luella said, and followed Mellie toward the house.

"All this stuff is for us?" Bailey asked in amazement as he eyed the back end of his parents' pickup.

Henry nodded. "Folks in this town think a lot of you and Mellie." Henry smiled. "I'm proud, son. Of you...and the place you've made for yourself here."

Warmth swept through Bailey at his father's words. Henry wasn't the type of man to throw compliments around casually. Bailey clapped his father on the back. "Come on, let's get this stuff unloaded. And please, Dad, don't lift anything heavy, otherwise Mom will have my head on a platter."

Henry grinned. "You've got that right."

It took the men about half an hour to get everything into the house and to the spare bedroom. Then they joined Mellie and Luella at the table for a cup of coffee.

As always Bailey fought a big dose of irritation as he listened to his parents disagree on everything from whether it was supposed to rain the next day to what kind of dog made the best pet.

He'd listened to the two of them for most of his life and had been appalled to discover Stephanie and him falling into the same pattern. They'd bickered about mealtimes, they'd argued about bedtime. Anything and everything became a point of contention. By the time she'd left, it had been almost a relief.

And that's why he'd sworn he would never, ever marry again. He refused to live his life as his parents had, so obviously miserable with each other.

His parents remained for about an hour, then left. He and Mellie ate ham sandwiches, then he headed back to the barn to work, leaving Mellie in charge of organizing the wedding gifts.

He worked in the barn until dinner time then ensured that all the pups were doing okay, and with his paperwork caught up, he headed back to the house.

Throughout the afternoon while he'd worked, he'd found himself playing and replaying in his head the conversation he and Mellie had been having just before his parents arrived.

He'd wanted...no, needed to make it clear to her that although he had been her first lover, he had no intention of being her last.

But, he hadn't been able to help being irritated by the fact that she'd said he would never be the kind of husband she wanted.

The conversation was still on his mind when he entered the house and smelled the luscious scent of Italian sauce. "Hmm, it smells great in here," he said as he closed the front door behind him.

"That's supper you smell."

Bailey followed her voice into the kitchen. As he stepped over the child gate, Squirt came racing toward him, his back end wiggling at a hundred miles an hour. He bent down and scratched the pup behind his ear.

Mellie turned from the stove, her cheeks flushed becomingly from the heat of her cooking. "You're just in time. By the time you wash up, I'll have it on the table."

"Great, I'm starving."

As Bailey washed his hands in the kitchen sink, Mellie scurried around to put the meal on the table. A few minutes later they were seated across from each other, helping themselves to the spaghetti and meatballs and salad she'd prepared.

"All the pups doing okay?" she asked.

"Yeah, they seem to be holding their own. In another week or two I need to put some posters up offering them to good homes."

"What's your schedule like for tomorrow?"

"I've got a couple of appointments in the morning," Bailey said. "Then, in the afternoon, I need to drive out to Jess Manning's place. He's got a calf that isn't doing very well and he wants me to take a look at it. Why? You have something in mind?"

"I figured I'd help you out in the morning, then head into town. I need to pick up some thank-you notes and get started on them, and after that I was going to unload some of the boxes I brought over from my apartment." She paused to swipe a dollop of sauce from her mouth, then continued. "Bailey, you won't believe some of the nice things people bought for us. Too bad we can't use them for the duration of our marriage, but of course we can't. It won't be long and we'll be returning them all."

"And everyone will think we're total failures," Bailey replied. His sentence was punctuated by a tiny bark from Squirt, who had been dancing under the table as if waiting for a morsel of food to drop through.

Mellie looked at him in surprise. "No, they won't," she protested. "Everyone will think it's wonderful that we were able to call an end to our marriage and still remain the best of friends." She took a bite of her spaghetti, then continued. "Besides, eventually I'll marry my dream man and he'll love me to distraction and we'll live happily ever after."

Bailey snorted. "You'd think that in all the years we've been friends I would have been able to convince you of the truth—that there is no happily-ever-after when it comes to marriages. But you continue to live in a fantasy despite my wanting to educate you to the truth."

She laughed. "You just wait, Bailey. Someday I'm going to find a man who loves me, a man I love, and he'll want a houseful of children and a porch swing," she added pointedly.

He laughed and reached for another piece of garlic bread. "The first time you see a porch swing hanging in front of my house, be looking for the men in white suits to escort me to the nearest insane asylum. A porch swing could only mean I've completely lost my mind."

"And that, my dear Bailey, is why you are my very best friend and not my dream man," Mellie replied.

Bailey nodded, relieved that the fact that they'd made love hadn't made her go all silly on him. Their plan was still intact, and after she got pregnant, they would part amicably and remain the best of friends for the rest of their lives.

They had just finished with the dishes when the doorbell rang. "I'll get it," Melanie said. She left the kitchen and hurried to the front door.

SueEllen Trexlor stood on the porch, a huge smile on her attractive face and a large box in her arms. "Hey, Melanie. I'm sorry I couldn't be at your wedding reception last night, but I thought I'd drop by and bring you and Bailey the present I bought for you."

"You didn't have to do that," Melanie protested.

"Well, of course I did." SueEllen's smile exposed most of her perfect, white teeth. "You and Bailey are two of my most favorite people in the whole wide world."

This, from a young woman who had never before given Melanie the time of day. Melanie had a feeling SueEllen wanted that Miss Dairy Cow crown badly enough to make nice with the judge's wife.

Melanie stepped aside to allow SueEllen to enter the living room. She raced over to the coffee table and set the box on top. "Whew, that's heavy."

Without the box in her arms, Melanie now saw that SueEllen was clad in a denim skirt the size of a cereal

CARLA CASSIDY

box and a midriff top that exposed an expanse of tanned, firm stomach.

"Bailey," Melanie yelled, wondering where he had disappeared to, "we have company."

He appeared from the direction of the bedrooms, and Melanie suspected his intent had been to hide from the big-haired brunette. But there was no way Melanie was going to entertain their guest alone.

"Look who's here," she exclaimed.

"Hi, SueEllen." Bailey offered her a faint smile and moved to Melanie's side, as if unconsciously seeking Melanie's protection against the big bad beauty queen wannabe.

"Hey, Bailey. So, how is married life treating you?"

"Fine...just fine." He threw an arm around Melanie's shoulder. "I've never been so happy."

SueEllen clapped her hands together. "Oh, I'm just so happy for you both. I just love it when the special people in my life find happiness together."

Special people in her life? Melanie fought the impulse to laugh. The only special person in SueEllen's life was SueEllen.

"I had to find the perfect gift for you," she continued as she moved to the large box on the coffee table. "It took most of my tips to buy it, but of course you both are worth it."

"Really, SueEllen, you shouldn't have. This really isn't necessary," Bailey protested as she ripped open the top of the box.

"Nonsense," she replied. She bent over to pick up whatever was in the box, her skirt riding high enough to show the edges of hot-pink underpanties.

Melanie glanced at Bailey to see if he was taking in the view, but his gaze was focused on the front door, as if he would by thought and concentration alone send SueEllen back through it.

She pulled out what appeared to be a huge brightly decorated dog bowl. With her elbow she nudged the box off the table, then set the bowl in the center of the coffee table. "When I saw this in the store, it positively screamed your name," she said as she withdrew more items from the box.

"There's no way that thing screamed my name," Melanie muttered beneath her breath. Bailey nudged her in the ribs, his eyes sparkling with suppressed laughter.

"Melanie, could you be a dear and get me a big pitcher of water?"

"A pitcher of water?"

SueEllen nodded. "You'll see why I need it in a minute."

"Okay," Melanie agreed and left the living room for the kitchen. She filled a large pitcher with water, then returned to the living room where it was immediately obvious why she needed the water.

A tabletop fountain. It was the most ridiculous thing Melanie had ever seen. In the middle of the bowl was a mountain of ceramic dog biscuits in various colors. A ceramic German shepherd with a toothy grin played king of the mountain. Four fire hydrants rode the edges of the bowl.

SueEllen poured the pitcher of water into the bowl, then plugged in the fountain. Water spewed from the fire hydrants, hit the demented-looking German shepherd and he bobbed up and down.

SueEllen squealed and clapped her hands together. "Isn't that just too cute?"

"I am utterly speechless," Melanie said.

"You really shouldn't have, SueEllen," Bailey exclaimed.

"Of course I should have. And now I'll just get out of your hair. I'm sure you two have better things to do than entertain me." She headed for the front door, but before she reached it, turned back to Melanie. "Call me, Melanie, maybe we can do lunch." With these final words she flew through the door.

"That woman has never spoken more than two words to me, and now suddenly she wants to do lunch," Melanie exclaimed.

"Only one of the bonuses of being married to the judge of the Miss Dairy Cow Contest," Bailey replied with a grin.

"And the other bonuses would be?" Melanie raised one of her eyebrows inquisitively.

Bailey pointed to the fountain. "Works of art, right here in our living room."

Melanie laughed. "It's awful, isn't it. Do we really have to keep it in the center of the coffee table?"

"No, I'll take it out to the office in the barn. It will

be more appropriate there.'' He shoved his hands into his pockets. "So, you want to watch a movie before bedtime?"

"Sure," she agreed. Actually she was relieved with the suggestion. With the coming of darkness outside and SueEllen's departure, she was suddenly filled with a strange tension as she thought of the night to come, the first night she would sleep in Bailey's bed.

She went into the kitchen and grabbed Squirt, then returned to the living room where Bailey had turned on the television. He was already in his easy chair, remote in hand. She sank down on the sofa, Squirt in her lap.

The puppy wiggled for a minute or two, then settled, lulled by the stroking of her hand against his soft fur. Melanie tried to focus on the movie, but her mind refused to cooperate. Instead she found herself wondering about the night to come.

Would Bailey want to have sex again? Although she was eager to get pregnant, she wasn't sure she was up for lovemaking that night. To tell the truth, she had a bit of discomfort from their lovemaking that morning.

She'd never slept with a man in the same bed. She found herself wondering if Bailey snored. Was he a cover hog? Did he like to cuddle? By the time the movie was over, she was more nervous than she could remember being in a very long time.

It was ridiculous, she told herself, to be so nervous about sharing a bed with Bailey. They'd already made love, so there were certainly no more secrets between them. So, why was she nervous?

Bailey seemed utterly at ease, laughing at the appropriate places in the comedy he'd chosen to play. As she listened to his laughter, her nervous tension began to ebb.

She'd always loved the sound of his laughter, rich and robust, it had been the first thing she'd noticed about him when they'd both been seven years old. Even then his laughter had made her smile.

"You ready to call it a day?" he asked when the movie was over.

"Sure," she said, and rose from her chair. She took Squirt out through the screened-in porch off the kitchen and set him in the grass to do his business. When he was finished, she made sure the potty pads were clean on the porch. Squirt didn't quite have a handle on the notion of potty training.

By the time she'd settled Squirt down and returned to the living room, Bailey had already turned off the television and disappeared into the bedroom. Again a bit of nervousness knocked around in her stomach.

When she entered the bedroom, Bailey was already in bed. "You don't eat crackers in bed or talk in your sleep or anything else weird, do you?" he asked.

She laughed. "I was just wondering the same kinds of things about you."

"No strange sleeping habits here," he replied. He turned off his bedside lamp, leaving the lamp on her side of the bed to cast a soft, golden glow in the room.

Melanie, remembering that her sleeping attire was in the spare room, raced across the hall, grabbed her things, then returned to the master bedroom.

"Bailey," she began hesitantly from the adjoining bathroom door. "Are we going to..."

"Not tonight," he replied quickly. "I know you're eager to get pregnant, but it probably wouldn't be that comfortable for you tonight." His gaze didn't quite meet hers.

"You're right," she agreed. "I'll be ready for bed in just a few minutes." She disappeared into the privacy of the bathroom.

She decided on a quick shower, then dressed in her silk camisole and tap pants. She captured her unruly hair into a neat braid, then grabbed a bottle of her favorite lotion and returned to the bedroom.

Bailey appeared to be already asleep, stretched out on his stomach with his face turned away from her side of the bed.

She eased down to the bed and propped her pillow up behind her so she was half sitting, then opened her lotion and began to apply it on her arms.

The sweet scent of wildflowers filled the room, and she'd just begun to apply the lotion on her legs when Bailey rolled over and looked at her.

She thought his eyes flared wide for just a moment. "What are you doing?"

"Every night before I go to bed I put lotion on so my skin will be soft."

"Your skin is plenty soft enough," he said, and Melanie thought he sounded irritated.

"Am I bothering you?" She closed the lid on the lotion and set it on the nightstand. "I'm sorry."

"You aren't bothering me, I was just wondering what you were doing." His eyes appeared darker than usual. "Do you always wear that to bed?"

Melanie stared at him for a moment. He was looking at her as if she were some sort of strange alien. "And what's wrong with what I wear to bed?" she demanded.

"Nothing," he said hurriedly, a slight flush sweeping over his face. "I just assumed you were a T-shirt kind of sleeper."

"Then I guess you assumed wrong," she replied. She turned off her lamp, plunging the room into a profound darkness. "It's one of my deep, dark secrets, Bailey," she said softly.

"What is?"

"That I'm more of a silk and satin woman than people think I am. What about you? Do you have any deep, dark secrets that you hide from everyone?"

"Yeah, mine is that I don't like chitchat when I'm trying to go to sleep."

"Well, excuse me," Melanie exclaimed, and tried to ignore the swift pain his words created. "I guess your other deep, dark secret is that you're a jerk right before you go to sleep." She yanked the covers up over her and turned her back to him.

She had no idea what had riled him, but if this was the way he acted at bedtime, she was more than grateful this whole marriage thing was just a temporary arrangement.

Chapter Eight

Bailey awoke with the tantalizing fragrance of flowers filling his senses. Warm curves filled his arms and
something tickled at his nose.

He opened his eyes to find the room in whisper-
soft shades of dawn. Mellie's back was to him, her
body spoon fashion against his. Tendrils of her hair
had escaped the confining braid while she slept and
that's what tickled his face.

One of his arms was thrown over her, as if to capture her and keep her tight against him. He didn't
remember reaching for her in the night, but it was
obvious he had.

He thought about moving, but she was sleeping so
peacefully he hated to take the chance of disrupting
her sleep. Instead, he closed his eyes and thought

about those moments just before she'd turned out her light.

When he'd smelled the scent of her lotion and turned around to see what she was doing, the sight of her in the sexy, beige silk nightclothes had shocked him.

Mellie had always been a T-shirt and jeans kind of woman. When she wore dresses, they were usually rather shapeless and distinctly unsexy. But she liked silk and satin, and that added a whole new dimension to the woman who had been his best friend for most of his life.

And that's what had made him cranky the night before. He'd felt as if a stranger had crawled into his bed, and he didn't like it. He didn't like it one bit.

With the body-warmed silk of her minuscule nightclothes smooth against his skin and the scent of her stirring in his head, he felt his body responding, and that's when he decided to get out of the bed.

As gently as possible he lifted his arm from around her and slid out from beneath the covers. She didn't move when he got out of the bed and went into the bathroom.

Moments later as he stood beneath a hot shower he thought again of his first glimpse of Mellie in her silk. For a brief moment, white-hot desire had roared through him. That had been what had thrown him for a loop.

He wasn't supposed to want Mellie, that hadn't

been part of their deal. He *had* to make love to her in order to fulfill his part of their bargain, but desire wasn't supposed to enter into the agreement.

By the time he got out of the shower, he had chalked his momentary desire for Mellie up to an anomaly, a weird chemical reaction that wasn't likely to happen again, except of course for the appropriate reason of procreation.

She was still asleep after he'd showered and dressed. He left the bedroom quietly and slipped into the kitchen to make the coffee.

As the coffee brewed, Bailey moved to stand in front of the window that faced the back of his property. This was his favorite time of the day, when dawn chased the night shadows off his property and gave everything—the green grass, the cherry and apple trees, even the old shed in the distance, a luster of gold.

He'd mortgaged his soul for this house and the hundred acres of property that went with it. It had been the biggest gamble of his life, a gamble that had paid off. As the only vet in the town of Foxrun, business was booming.

He was sitting at the table and working on his second cup of coffee when Mellie came into the kitchen. Her hair was in a neat braid and she was clad in worn jeans and a green T-shirt that perfectly matched the color of her eyes.

"Good morning, Mr. Grouchy," she said as she headed across the kitchen for the coffee.

"I was a bit cranky last night, wasn't I?" he agreed. "Sorry about that. I guess you can chalk it up to overtiredness and the last of my hangover."

"And I accept your apology." She joined him at the table with a cup of coffee. "After I help you with the pups, I'm going to head into town. I need to buy those thank-you notes and get started on them and I also need to pick up some groceries. Those questionable casseroles look interesting, but they've been in the fridge long enough that they need to be thrown out."

"I'll buy the groceries." He grinned at her. "It's what a husband does. If you go to Quigley's you can just charge it to my account."

She nodded and sipped at her coffee.

"Did you sleep well?" He wondered if she knew how their bodies had found each other in the night.

"Like a dead person. I don't think I moved all night long."

She had moved all right...right into his arms, right against his body. But if she didn't remember it, he certainly wasn't going to tell her about it. He finished his coffee and stood.

"I guess I'll head on out to the barn and get a jump on the day." He rinsed his cup and put it into the dishwasher, then leaned down and scratched Squirt behind his ears.

"I'll just make up the bed and clean up Squirt's potty pads on the back porch, then be out to help you."

"Take your time," he replied, then headed out the door.

The sun was already warm overhead, and as he entered the barn he was greeted with excited yipping and meowing from the various residents.

He booted up the computer and brought up his daily schedule and records for all the animals he was currently treating. He had two morning appointments, a yearly exam and shots for a malamute named Blue, and a follow-up visit with a little Pomeranian named Gizmo, who'd suffered a broken leg four weeks before. Later that afternoon he had a calf to check. In the meantime there were puppies and cats to feed and examine.

He'd examined four puppies by the time Mellie joined him. He put her to work feeding the critters, then went back to his examinations.

As they worked, they fell into a lively discussion about local politics. Bailey had always found Mellie's spirited opinions stimulating, and they'd always been able to argue good-naturedly and without any rancor.

They had just finished with the exams and feeding of the dogs, and he was in the middle of detailing why the town needed a new mayor when the crunch of gravel in the driveway signaled the arrival of a car.

"That must be Max with Blue," he said. He

washed his hands at the sink, then went to the door, Mellie just behind him.

Bailey frowned as he saw the unfamiliar car in the drive. As they watched, a young boy climbed out of the passenger seat, a shoebox in his hand.

"That's Jimmy Sinclair," Mellie said. "He was in my class this year."

"I've never treated any of their animals. Wonder what he's doing here?"

Together he and Mellie walked out of the barn and met Jimmy as he approached them. "Hi, Jimmy," Mellie greeted the youngster.

"Hi, Miss Watters—I mean, Mrs. Jenkins," the boy corrected himself. "My mom brung me out here 'cause Whiskers died and she said Dr. Jenkins knows what to do."

Bailey smiled at Jimmy and knelt down on one knee. "Is Whiskers in the shoebox?" he asked gently.

Jimmy nodded, his brown eyes sparkling far too brightly, and gripped the shoebox more tightly against his chest.

"Could I take a look at Whiskers?" Bailey asked.

Jimmy hesitated just a moment, then nodded and held the box out to Bailey. Bailey slid the top off and peered inside. Sure enough, there was one dead golden hamster on top of a bedding of tissue.

Bailey knew how devastating the loss of a pet could be, and it didn't matter if that pet was a dog, a cat, a hamster or a goldfish. He'd created a place to bury beloved pets to help people put some closure to their grief.

He placed the lid back on the box then handed it to Jimmy. "I've got a special place to take Whiskers. While I get a shovel, you might tell your mom we're going for a little walk and will be back in a few minutes."

As Jimmy ran to tell his mother, Bailey went into the barn and grabbed a shovel. A moment later Jimmy, Bailey and Mellie set off walking down the lane.

Bailey placed his free hand on Jimmy's shoulder as they walked. "How long did you have Whiskers?"

"Since I was six. I'm almost eight now," Jimmy replied. "He was fine last night when I went to bed. He was running on his wheel. He did that sometimes at night. Then when I got up this morning, I went over to his cage to tell him good morning and he was dead."

Bailey squeezed his shoulder sympathetically. He was a cute kid, with a thatch of straw-colored hair and big, expressive brown eyes. "You know, Jimmy, hamsters don't live very long. I imagine Whiskers just died of old age."

"Really?" Jimmy looked up at him with trusting eyes. "I thought maybe I did something wrong, but I couldn't think of anything I done wrong."

"*Did* wrong," Mellie corrected the boy automatically.

"No," Bailey replied. "You know, Jimmy, I know about these things, and Whiskers definitely looked like he died from old age."

Jimmy sighed in obvious relief, and Mellie smiled at Bailey over Jimmy's head. It was a soft smile and Bailey tried not to notice how the sunshine stroked brilliant fires into her red hair, making it look achingly touchable.

They walked past the blackberry bushes and the pond and through a pasture where two cows ignored their presence.

At the back of the pasture was a small grove of trees and a large plot of ground, all encircled by a white picket fence. Bailey opened the fence and escorted Jimmy and Mellie into the peaceful, shady area.

"This is the place where we say goodbye to pets who have died," Bailey said. "Is there a special place you'd like me to put Whiskers?"

Jimmy looked around the area, where here and there were wooden markers noting the resting places of other beloved pets.

"How about there?" He pointed to a spot beneath one of the trees.

Bailey squeezed his shoulder once again. "That looks like a great place for a hamster," he agreed. "Was Whiskers a good hamster?" Bailey asked as he began to dig.

Jimmy shrugged. "Sure, he was good." He hesitated a moment then added, "'Cept sometimes he would bite me kind of hard. Then once I got him out of his cage and let him sit on my bed, only he ran away and I couldn't find him for a day and my mom was really, really mad."

Bailey hid his smile as he set the shovel aside. "Hamsters sometimes like to explore," he replied. "And that usually makes moms mad."

"Boy, are you telling me," Jimmy quipped with a pained expression.

Bailey gently took the box from the boy, noting that Mellie placed a hand on Jimmy's shoulder as if in support. "We'll just wrap him in the tissue paper and throw the box away, okay?"

Jimmy nodded solemnly and watched as Bailey placed the little critter into the hole he had dug. "You know, Jimmy. This isn't the last time you'll see Whiskers," Bailey said. "When you go to Heaven, Whiskers will be there waiting for you."

"Will he still sometimes bite my finger too hard?"

Bailey smiled and shook his head. "Oh, no. In Heaven pets never bite. Now, would you like to say a few words of goodbye to Whiskers?"

Jimmy nodded and solemnly moved closer to the small grave. "Goodbye, Whiskers. You were mostly a good hamster and I'll see you in Heaven."

For a moment Bailey thought Jimmy might cry, but although his eyes were once again overly shiny, he looked up at Bailey and nodded. Just as solemnly, Bailey shoveled dirt into the grave.

As they walked back toward the house, Bailey promised he would make a marker for Whiskers and that Jimmy was welcome to come and visit any time.

Mellie spent a few minutes discussing the next school year with the boy, then they both said hello to his mother and minutes later watched as Jimmy and his mom drove away.

Bailey started to turn back toward the barn, but sensed Mellie's gaze on him. "What?" he asked.

She shrugged her slender shoulders and sighed. "I was just thinking that it's a shame you don't want children, because you would be an awesome daddy." She didn't wait for his reply but turned and headed toward the house.

A week and a half. She had been married for a whole week and a half. Melanie turned the faucet to add more hot water to her bath and sank lower in the scented water.

Bailey was outside finishing up chores and when he came in and cleaned up they were going into town for supper. It would be their first meal out since they'd gotten married.

But it wasn't the outing that weighed heavily on her mind. That day she'd received in the mail her contract from the school. All it needed was her signature and she would once again be teaching second grade in the fall.

The problem was, she wasn't sure if she should sign it or not. If she immediately became pregnant with Bailey's baby then she would deliver in March and have two full months of school left. She didn't want to have a baby and have to return to work.

On the other hand, if she didn't sign it and she didn't get pregnant right away, she would sit home with little to do, and eat into the savings she'd put away for when she had a baby.

As if the contract problem wasn't enough, she had a bigger concern weighing on her mind. She picked up the bath sponge and swiped it down her throat.

She thought she might be a nymphomaniac.

The word resonated inside her brain as she finished her bath. The idea that she might be one had grown through the past week. She and Bailey had made love almost every night, and it worried her that she liked it. She liked it a lot.

Bath finished, she stood and reached for a towel, her mind filled with thoughts of making love to Bailey. She wasn't supposed to like it. It was simply supposed to be a means to an end.

But she loved the way Bailey's warm body felt against hers, she loved the taste of his lips. And more than anything she loved how he made her feel when they were joined in passion.

It worried her that when they finished making love,

all she could think about was the anticipation of the next time they would make love.

It couldn't be because of Bailey himself. She had no romantic feelings toward him. She couldn't have, because that might mess up the beautiful friendship they shared. And that meant she loved sex.

She must be a nymphomaniac.

She shoved this troubling thought aside as she dressed in a pair of beige slacks and a beige and emerald-green blouse she'd never worn before.

It would be nice to get out. She and Bailey had always enjoyed eating at the café and she was looking forward to the outing.

She had just finished fixing her hair when Bailey walked in, bringing with him the scent of the outdoors. His blue eyes flared slightly at the sight of her. "You look...nice." His voice held the faintest touch of surprise.

"It's not every day my husband decides to take me out to dinner," she began, and in the back of her mind realized his facial expression had irritated her. "I figured it was a momentous, spiff-up kind of deal, but if you prefer I'll pull on a pair of old, dirty jeans and a ripped T-shirt so you won't be quite so surprised."

"Jeez, Mellie, all I did was give you a compliment, don't bite off my head." He pulled his T-shirt off over his head, exposing his muscular torso.

Instantly she wanted to run her fingers through his thatch of chest hair, press herself into the warmth and security of his body. This only sent her irritation up a notch and brought home what she had worried about only moments before.

"Bailey." She sat on the edge of the bed. "Can I ask you a question?"

"Anything...always," he replied, and sat down next to her to take off his shoes.

She bit her bottom lip thoughtfully before continuing. He was her best friend. Surely she could talk about anything with him...even the possibility that she was sexually insatiable.

"Do you know any nymphomaniacs?"

He gasped and nearly fell off the bed. "Excuse me?"

Melanie felt a blush warming her cheeks. "You heard me."

"I heard you but I can't believe what I just heard."

The heat that had swept across her cheeks now crept down her throat. "I just wanted to know if you know any and if they're normal in every other area of their life except for that."

"Mellie, what's going on in your crazy head?" he asked, his oh, so blue eyes holding her gaze.

She broke eye contact with him, suddenly embarrassed that she'd even brought it up. "Never mind," she said.

He laughed. "Oh, no, you don't. You can't bring up a topic like that and say 'never mind.' Now, what's going on?" She met his gaze and to her horror felt tears welling up. He took her hands in his. "Mellie, honey, what's wrong?"

She tried to laugh, but it came out as a strangled sob. "I think I'm a nymphomaniac!"

He stared at her, obviously stunned, then thew his head back and roared with laughter.

"It's not funny," she protested, laughing and crying at the same time. "I...I think I might be one."

He released her hands to wipe tears of laughter from his eyes. "Why on earth would you think that?"

She fought for composure, unsure if tears or laughter would escape. "Bailey, I like making love. I like it a lot."

"I like making love, too," he replied, his eyes sparkling with obvious amusement. "I like it a lot. Does that make me a nymphomaniac?"

"No, from what I understand, that just makes you a male," she replied dryly. She stood. "Just forget I brought it up."

"I don't want to forget it." He took hold of her arm and pulled her back to the bed next to him. "I think we should explore this further." His eyes were still filled with mirth and his dimple flashed near his mouth.

She yanked her arm from his hold and crossed both arms over her chest. "Go take your shower. You're just making fun of me," she exclaimed.

He stood, that sexy grin of his lifting the corners of his mouth. "I'm just teasing you a little, Mellie."

His voice was gentle. "Trust me, it's normal and healthy to enjoy the act of making love, especially when the man you're making love with is such an expert in the field." He winked broadly then ducked as she threw his dirty T-shirt at him. His laughter filled the room even after he'd disappeared into the bathroom.

Chapter Nine

It was a week before the Fourth of July and the Miss Dairy Cow Contest along with all the other activities that would take place on that day, and the whole town of Foxrun had gone dairy cow crazy.

As Bailey drove down Main Street, cows were everywhere. Papier maché cows peeked out of store windows, life-size statues stood on the sidewalks and flags in the likeness of bovines hung from every streetlamp.

Bailey was meeting Tanner for coffee at the café in a few minutes. He hadn't seen his neighbor since before his wedding to Mellie and was looking forward to a little man talk.

If he was perfectly honest with himself, he would face the fact that he'd made the arrangement to meet

Tanner because he needed some time away from the house...away from Mellie.

A little more than a month of marriage had trans-formed his bachelor pad into an alien landscape. Lacy doilies now decorated the surface of his end tables, and most evenings fragrant candles filled the air with the scent of summer breezes and wildflowers, straw-berries and apples.

In the kitchen, colorful potholders had appeared, matching the pretty dish towels and brightening up what had been comfortably utilitarian.

The bedroom and master bath were the worst of all. Her scent lingered in the very molecules of the air, taunting him each time he entered either room.

Who would have thought Mellie's hair would have been so soft? Who would have believed her skin would be like warm silk? And who would have imag-ined that she'd be such a responsive, fiery lover?

He shoved all these disturbing thoughts aside as he spied an empty parking space in front of the shop belonging to Tanner's wife, Colette. At least the Little Bit Boutique had no cows in the window. Instead the window held a yellow-canopied crib with a cheerful, smiling teddy bear.

As Bailey got out of his car, Tanner walked out of the shop, a smile of greeting on his face. "I'll just be a few minutes, I've got some boxes to unload, then we can get coffee." He motioned to the shop. "Come on in and say hello to the boss."

Bailey hesitated only a minute, unsure if he wanted

to enter the place devoted to babies. Every time he thought of Mellie having his child, his head filled with enough confusing thoughts to give him a headache.

Still, he followed Tanner in, instantly noticing the baby-powder scent of the shop. Colette stood behind a register, ringing up a female customer Bailey didn't recognize. She smiled and waved at him.

"I'll be in the back room for just a couple of minutes," Tanner said. "Feel free to wander around and look things over." He disappeared toward the back of the store.

Bailey shoved his hands in his pockets and meandered up an aisle that displayed a variety of little bitty clothing. Were babies really that small? He touched the lace of a tiny dress and tried to imagine his daughter clad in it.

His daughter.

Would she have a spill of curly red hair like her mother, or dark hair like his? Would her eyes be blue or green or an intriguing combination of both? As she got older, would she be a princess or a tomboy?

A tiny baseball uniform brought the same kind of questions to his mind. What would his son be like? Would he miss the presence of a full-time father in his life? Would a daughter?

"Amazing, isn't it?"

He turned around to see Colette. "What?"

She touched the little ball uniform. "The items they make for babies nowadays. Look at this." She opened a drawer and pulled out a pair of name-brand tennis shoes no bigger than his fingers.

"Unbelievable," he said. "The shop looks great. Is business going well?"

Her eyes sparkled brightly. "Better than I dreamed. Apparently babies are big business in Foxrun. In fact, I've been wondering why you and Melanie haven't stopped in to visit yet."

"We've been pretty busy lately," he replied.

"Oh, yes, we heard about the puppy mill. Are the puppies all doing okay?"

Bailey smiled. "Healthy and thriving, and I've managed to adopt out four in the past two weeks. You and Tanner in the market for a puppy?"

"I don't know. It might be nice. We have Bugsy, but he's pretty much an outdoor dog. It might be nice to have a sweet, indoor dog. I'd have to talk it over with Tanner." Her smile grew larger. "You see, we just found out yesterday that there's going to be an addition to our family."

At that moment Tanner appeared next to her and threw an arm over her shoulder. "I can tell by the smile on her face she just told you our news."

"She did. Congratulations to you both." For just a moment Bailey envied the utter happiness that shone from his old friend's eyes. "Who would have thought the most confirmed bachelor of Foxrun would not only be married but starting a family of his own?"

Tanner laughed. "And who would have thought the second most confirmed bachelor in Foxrun would be married and in the process of starting his family," he replied.

Bailey wanted to protest, to tell Tanner their situations were entirely different. Tanner was in his marriage for life, Bailey was in his marriage for mutual convenience and when the Miss Dairy Cow Contest was over and Mellie got pregnant, Bailey intended to go back to his carefree single life.

"Yeah, I guess in every man's life there comes a time when it's important to grow up and realize what's important...like love and family." Tanner kissed Colette on the forehead. "And now I'm going to regress a bit and go have coffee with Bailey, where we'll probably talk about fast cars and faster babes."

Both men laughed as Colette shot an elbow into Tanner's ribs. "Go on, get out of here, both of you," she exclaimed.

Coffee with Tanner was pleasant. They spoke of their farms and their respective businesses. Tanner's place, Two Hearts, was not only known for prime Charolais and Hereford cattle, but also for the quarter horses he'd been breeding.

They talked about what farms were thriving in the area and which appeared to be failing and why. They laughed about old times and spoke of old friends.

Bailey would have enjoyed himself completely had he been able to get the mental image of his yet-to-be-conceived baby out of his head.

He'd thought he would get Mellie pregnant as his end of the deal, then return to the easy friendship they had shared and he'd cherished for years. In his mind he'd assumed he would take the position of a favorite uncle to the baby she'd bear.

"I can't wait until this contest is over," he said as he and Tanner walked from the café back to where Bailey had parked his truck.

"The town does go a little nuts, doesn't it," Tanner replied.

"It's not the town, it's the people. Two days ago Madge Walker brought her granddaughter in to see me. The granddaughter is only about ten or twelve. Anyway, apparently she's a little contestant in the making and wanted me to see her talent...just as kind of a trial run for when she gets old enough to enter the contest."

"And?" Tanner raised a dark brow, his features radiating amusement.

"And so reluctantly I agreed. Before I know it, the young lady whipped out two batons, lit them on fire and threw them up in the air. The smoke alarms went off, the dogs went nuts and I thought Madge Walker was going to have a heart attack in the middle of my barn."

Tanner laughed. "Just think, Bailey, this time next year this will all be nothing more than a vague memory."

"Yeah, but I have a feeling I'm going to have a lot of nightmares in the next week," Bailey replied ruefully.

A few minutes later as he drove back to his ranch,

his thoughts once again turned to Mellie and the baby she would eventually carry. For the first time since he and Mellie had struck their deal, he realized he wanted more.

He simply wasn't the type of man who could walk away from his child and merely exist around the edges of his or her life.

It was time to have a talk with Mellie. He needed to make her understand that he would not be shoved into the background of their child's life.

"Mellie," he called as he entered the front door. There was no reply. He walked down the hallway and peeked into each of the bedrooms but saw no sign of her.

As he went into the kitchen, he caught sight of her outside the window. She was playing with Squirt in the backyard. Clad in one of her shapeless sundresses, she was running with Squirt nipping and yipping at her heels.

Despite the nonformfitting nature of her dress, he could mentally "see" her shape—the graceful slenderness of her back, the upward thrust of her breasts and the long length of her legs. She looked beautiful with the sun sparking on her hair and laughter warming her features.

Desire soared through him...thick and hot. He wanted her, right there...in the grass with the sun warming them and the scent of her riding the summer breeze. He wanted to tangle his hands in the thick

spill of her curly hair and feel her warm body next
to his.

As always, irritation came with the desire. What
was it about Melanie Watters that made him want her
so? How could he want a woman he didn't love romantically?

He had a feeling what he was about to tell her
would make her mad. She'd chosen him to father her
child, knowing he'd never wanted children. She'd obviously expected that he would be happy to be rele-
gated to friend-of-the-family status.

Better get it over with, he thought as he walked
onto the back porch, then opened the back door.
"Melanie, we need to talk," he said without preamble.

She scooped Squirt up in her arms. "Hmm, must
be serious. I can't remember the last time you called
me Melanie. You want to go inside?"

"No, we can talk here."

She gazed at him for a moment. "Just let me put
Squirt away, then you'll have my complete, undivided
attention."

As she carried Squirt back to the house, Bailey
sank down in the lush grass and waited for her. As
he waited for her, he thought again of those moments
in Colette's shop, when the nebulous idea of a child
had suddenly become the reality of *his* child.

She returned a moment later and sat facing him,
her slender, freckled legs stretching toward him.

"What's up?" she asked. "You look far too serious for such a gorgeous summer day."

Bailey thought for a moment, wondering how best to broach the subject of joint custody. "You know I've always told you I didn't want children."

She narrowed her eyes. "Don't tell me you're going to try to renege on our deal."

"No, not renege," he explained. "But, I want to modify."

A tiny frown furrowed her brow. "Modify how?"

He looked away, unwilling to hold her gaze. "I'll still try to get you pregnant, and we'll still divorce just as we planned, but I can't walk away from my child. I want joint custody."

He looked back at her, expecting to see anger shooting from her spring-green eyes. Instead, she smiled, one of her soft, gentle smiles that made his heart flip-flop uncomfortably in his chest.

"I'm not surprised," she said. "I've been expecting you to come to that conclusion."

"How could you have been expecting it? I didn't know until just a few minutes ago."

She stood, that wonderful smile still curving her lips. "I know what kind of man you are, Bailey. It's one of the reasons I wanted you to be the father of my baby—because I knew when it actually came down to it, you aren't the type of man to just turn your back and walk away. And now I'm going to go in and make some lunch. Are you coming?"

"I'll be there in just a minute or two," he said,

and remained seated in the grass. He needed to sit and think for a moment and try to figure out how it was possible that Melanie Watters apparently knew him better than he knew himself.

"Don't forget we're supposed to meet Mom and Dad at eleven by the barbecue stand for lunch," Melanie reminded Bailey as they drove toward the fairgrounds.

Finally the day had arrived. The Fourth of July had dawned with clear skies and the promise of a hot day. Bailey was in an exuberant mood, knowing that within hours his job as contest judge would be behind him.

Melanie also felt the excitement of the day. There was nothing quite like the Foxrun Fourth of July celebration. The fairground was transformed into a carnival complete with edge-of-your-seat rides, mouth-watering offers of a variety of food, and games of skill and chance. The celebration would end with a spectacular fireworks display.

"The contest isn't scheduled until five this evening, so we'll have basically all day to hang out and enjoy the fun," Bailey said.

Melanie nodded and stared out the truck window, trying not to dwell on how utterly handsome Bailey looked. Although he wore his usual tight-fitting jeans, his short-sleeved dress shirt had a blue-and-silver stripe that emphasized the startling blue of his eyes.

Melanie had tried to dress a little differently for the

day. She'd spied a cute sundress in the window of one of the boutiques in town and, after trying it on, had bought it.

The dress was more fitted than she was accustomed to wearing, but the color and style had called to her. The persimmon color accentuated her hair and almost perfectly matched her freckles. The bodice clung to her, the scoop neck toying with a bit of cleavage. The short, flirty skirt made her feel feminine and fun and pretty.

She wished she could capture forever the look in Bailey's eyes when she'd exited the bathroom in the dress. He'd emitted a deep wolf whistle, and there had been a spark in his eyes that had weakened her knees.

She looked back at him, realizing he'd been humming the tune of an old fifties song. "What are you thinking about?"

He flashed her a quick smile. "Just looking forward to the day." His smile deepened, flashing his charming dimple. "Every year I always love to see you stuff yourself with cotton candy and hot dogs and funnel cakes so you can whine about your sick tummy all through the fireworks display."

"I don't whine," she protested with a laugh.

His smile fell away. "You're right." He turned his attention back to his driving. "You aren't a whiner." He paused a moment, then continued. "My mother can be a whiner, and Stephanie...she was the queen of the whiners." Melanie said nothing, unsure how to respond. She'd always felt that Stephanie was a taboo topic with him.

"She woke up in the mornings whining that my bed was too soft and the room was too warm. Then it was the toast was too done, the coffee was weak and things would be different if we moved to the city and I'd become a real doctor."

She reached out her hand and placed it on his arm. "I'm sorry, Bailey."

He quirked an eyebrow as if in surprise. "Why should you be sorry?"

"Because you're my friend, and things didn't work out and you loved her." Funny, a twinge of something remarkably like jealousy crackled through her. She shoved the odd feeling away as Bailey continued talking.

"You know what they say—marry in haste, repent in leisure. I don't think I was ever really in love with Stephanie. I had a bad case of lust, and before I knew it we were married."

"Well, if it's any consolation, I don't think the bed is too soft at all," she replied in an attempt to lighten the suddenly solemn tone of the conversation.

Bailey laughed and gazed at her affectionately. "Every person on earth should have a good friend like you, Mellie."

She knew he meant the words as the best kind of compliment, but for some crazy reason they left her feeling rather empty inside.

As the fairgrounds came into view, she focused on

nothing else except the magic of her hometown's special celebration of the national holiday.

Melanie and Bailey had shared the fun of the carnival since they had been thirteen years old and their parents had finally allowed them to go on their own.

They bee-lined for the carousel. The colorful, lively looking mechanical horses always provided their first ride of the day. From there they went to several of the other rides, pausing in the fun only long enough to eat a funnel cake.

It was a day of fun, shared with friends, family and neighbors. Laughter was the rule of the day, and more than once the sound of Bailey's unbridled deep laughter caused a shiver of pleasure to race through Melanie.

They met Marybeth and Red Watters for lunch, dining on dripping spicy ribs and greasy fries. Within minutes Bailey's parents also joined them.

When five o'clock arrived and it was time for the contest, the bleachers in front of the stage area filled to see the beauty and talent of the young Foxrun women.

Melanie sat on the first row of the bleachers, grinning at Bailey who was seated on a chair of honor on stage. He looked as ill at ease as she'd ever seen him.

As she watched the pageant, she found herself thinking of the past several weeks of their marriage. There was a new intimacy between them that was both exhilarating and slightly frightening.

They touched often, in the intimate fashion of real

married couples. He'd taken to cuddling with her on the sofa at night as they watched movies. She would sometimes lie with her head in his lap and he'd toy with her hair or absently rub her shoulder and she'd know a contentment she'd never felt before in her life.

Their passionate lovemaking hadn't ebbed in the past month. Their physical unions remained breathtakingly beautiful for her, and afterward they often remained in each other's arms, talking softly in the darkness of their room. She pulled her thoughts away from her marriage as SueEllen Trexlor took the stage for her talent competition. She watched in amusement as SueEllen tap-danced, threatening to blacken both her eyes with her jiggling breasts each time she shuffled off to Buffalo.

SueEllen had called her several times over the past week, trying to set up a lunch date with her. It was only when Melanie told her that despite being married to the judge, she had no influence over him, that SueEllen stopped calling.

The surprise of the pageant was a pretty young woman named Susan Sanforth. Melanie knew Susan as a rather shy, young woman who worked in the local feedstore. But onstage she delivered a song in the voice of an angel, and during the interview portion showed an intelligence and wit that ultimately earned her the title of Miss Dairy Cow.

It was just after dusk when she and Bailey retrieved a blanket from the back of their truck, then hiked away from the fairgrounds. They were headed to the isolated, tree-laden area from which they had always watched the fireworks.

"Remind me if SueEllen drops off a casserole any-time soon not to take a bite of it. It will probably be laced with arsenic," Bailey said as they walked.

Melanie laughed. "With the look she gave you when you made your announcement, I don't think you have to worry about her ever speaking or cooking for you again."

"Good. She's been a major player in my night-mares lately."

She laughed again and looped her arm through his, enjoying the scent of his familiar cologne mingling with sunshine and the outdoors.

When they reached their destination, a copse of trees on a small rise some distance from the fair-grounds, Bailey spread out the blanket and they stretched out side by side, facing each other.

For a long moment neither of them spoke. Around them night began to fall, lengthening the shadows be-neath the trees as the sun completely disappeared from sight.

"You should wear dresses like that more often," he said, breaking the companionable silence.

She frowned. "Dresses like what?"

"Ones that, you know, show off what a nice shape you have."

A warm breeze of pleasure swept through her at his words. "You think I have a nice shape?"

"Stop fishing for compliments," he replied with a

grin. "If you stopped wearing those baggy dresses, you'd get so many compliments, I'd probably have to fight the men off you."

She laughed, the warmth turning into a thrill. "I guess old habits die hard. When I was young and everyone in school would call me skinny, minny Melanie, I always wore my clothes too big because I thought it would make me look fatter."

"Trust me, Mellie, nobody would mistake you for skinny, minny Mellie anymore."

The look in his eyes assured her for the first time in her life that she'd truly outgrown the skinny, freckle-faced redhead that people had often made fun of.

"Lunch was fun," she said, changing the subject.

Bailey's forehead furrowed. "It was fun until my folks started their usual bickering. How can two adults actually manage to cause such a stir over whether ribs should be parboiled or not?"

Melanie smiled. "Bailey, you take your parents bickering far too seriously. It's obvious they adore each other and their bickering is simply a form of affection."

"So you say," he replied dryly. "Personally, I think their constant bickering is the result of their unhappiness. But I don't want to talk about that now." He leaned forward and captured a curl of her hair. "What I want to do is relax and dwell in the aftermath of an almost perfect day."

"An almost perfect day?" She raised an eyebrow. "What could possibly make it any more perfect?"

"We've got about half an hour or so before the fireworks display begins." He trailed a finger down her face and across her lips, the light in his eyes a wicked blaze.

Melanie's mouth grew dry and her pulse quickened. "Why, Mr. Jenkins, what could you possibly have in mind?"

"Nothing more than a little tumble in the grass with Mrs. Jenkins."

It was at that moment when his mouth found hers that two horrible, heartbreaking realizations leaped into her mind. She was in love with Bailey Jenkins, and her period was a little more than a week late.

Chapter Ten

For the rest of her life, Melanie would remember making love to Bailey while the pyrotechnics display lit up the sky overhead and her love for him illuminated every corner of her heart.

Be careful what you wish for...it just might come true. The old adage whirled through her head as, with trembling fingers, she removed the pregnancy test from the drugstore sack.

Bailey was out in the barn, and she knew he had several appointments and probably wouldn't be returning to the house for at least an hour. It was a perfect time for her to take the pregnancy test. She'd already put it off long enough.

It had been a week since the Fourth of July celebration, and her period was now over two weeks late.

She'd put off taking the test, but knew it was unfair to wait any longer.

She took the test instrument out of the factory packaging, wishing she could go back and change all the rules. She wished they hadn't agreed that once she got pregnant they would divorce.

But nothing Bailey had said or done in the almost eight weeks of their marriage had indicated that he wanted to change this particular part of their agreement. He wanted joint custody of the baby she might be carrying, but he also wanted a divorce.

She took the test, then leaned against the sink and waited for the results. The package had said that within three minutes she would have an answer.

As she waited, her mind drifted back over the past week. In the last seven days she'd spent every moment loving Bailey and memorizing everything about him that she'd always taken for granted.

His beautiful smile with his dashing dimple was now emblazoned in her brain, along with the silver-blue flash of his eyes as he made love to her.

How had everything gotten so messed up? She wasn't supposed to have fallen in love with him. Why had he made it so impossible for her not to love him?

She had somehow thought she would be safe from falling in love with Bailey because of the strong, caring friendship they shared. But apparently that friendship had become the basis for something deeper, something more profound, and something utterly shattering.

It was time to check the test. If she was pregnant the test stick would turn pink. If she wasn't pregnant it would turn blue.

Drawing a deep breath, she peeked at the test stick. There, a bright-pink square stared at her.

Instantly her hands shot to her stomach as a wave of joy fluttered through her. Pregnant. She was pregnant with Bailey's baby.

The unbridled joy that soared through her ebbed, tainted by the realization that their deal was done. The pageant was over and she was pregnant. It was time for her to leave Bailey's house, leave their marriage.

Maybe she should take another test in a week or so. She'd heard these tests could sometimes give false positive reads. But even as the thought flittered through her mind she realized she wouldn't wait another week and wouldn't take another test.

If she did wait a week, she would only be putting off the inevitable. The inevitable would be painful whether it was accomplished today or a week from today.

It isn't the end of the world, she told herself as she began to pack her personal items in boxes. It wasn't as if she wouldn't ever see Bailey again. Surely they could go back to the special relationship they'd had before the marriage took place.

She had almost all of her things packed and by the door when Bailey came in late that afternoon. He stepped inside and gazed first at the boxes and suitcases, then at her. "What's all this?"

"All my stuff," she said, forcing a lightness in tone into her voice. "The deal is done, and if you'll help me get this stuff to my car, then I'll be out of your hair and you can go back to your bachelor ways."

"Whoa...slow down," he exclaimed. He swiped a hand through his hair and sank down on the sofa, his gaze not leaving hers. "You said the deal is done... does that mean...are you...?"

"Pregnant," she finished. "I'm pregnant." Saying the words aloud for the very first time sent a euphoric joy winging through her. "I took a home pregnancy test this morning and it came back positive."

"Mellie," he said softly, then he jumped up off the sofa and wrapped her in his arms. "My God, I can't believe it. We're actually pregnant."

Tears stung her eyes, and for a moment she buried her face in the front of his shirt, the familiar scent of him aching inside her.

He was so obviously pleased about the baby. A tiny ray of hope sprang up in her chest. Maybe now he would tell her to unpack, that she wasn't going anywhere because he loved her more than anything and wanted to be her husband for the rest of his life.

He released her, his gaze gentle and caring. "Mellie, you don't have to move out today. We can take the next couple of days and get you settled back into your place."

She took a step away from him, needing to escape his nearness as her hope died a painful death in her heart. This would have been the perfect time for him to rescind the terms of their agreement, to ask her to remain a part of his life as his wife.

Tears once again pressed hot and heavy behind her eyelids, but she drew a deep breath to maintain control. It wasn't fair of her to be upset, because she'd gotten exactly what she'd bargained for.

"I'd sort of been looking forward to getting back to my own life," she said. "I'd just as soon get this stuff loaded and sleep in my own bed tonight."

"Uh, okay...if that's what you want." His facial expression was inscrutable. "We'll load this stuff up, then I'll follow you to your apartment in my truck and help you unload it there."

"That's not necessary," she replied hurriedly. She suddenly felt the desperate need to escape him, before she mortified herself by breaking down.

"Of course it's necessary," he countered evenly. "I don't want you lifting anything heavy for the next nine months. Have you made a doctor's appointment yet?"

"Jeez, Bailey. I just took the test a couple of hours ago. I'll make a doctor's appointment later in the week."

"Let me know when it is and I'll go with you."

She nodded. "Will you take good care of Squirt?" Her gaze became blurry with tears as she thought of the little guy who had captured her heart from the moment she'd spied him in the back of the cattle truck.

Squirt barked from the kitchen at the sound of his

name. "Of course I'll take care of him," Bailey replied gently, obviously knowing how hard it was for her to leave him here. "But it's not like you're never going to see him again. We'll be seeing each other almost every day, and then there's our Friday movie nights."

She nodded. "I'm going to start to look around for a new place to live...someplace with a yard that allows pets." She picked up the lightest of the boxes, just wanting to get the move over with.

It took them nearly an hour to load up everything that Melanie had packed, then drive to her apartment.

"Whew, it's hot in here," Bailey said as he carried the first of the boxes into her place. "Why don't you open some windows while I get the rest of the things inside?"

As he returned to her car for more boxes, she turned on the air conditioner and went around opening windows to allow the escape of the stifling air.

It was amazing to her, that the place she had called home for the past seven years could feel so unhome-like. She didn't feel any relief or any joy in returning here. All she felt was the heavy weight of an aching heart.

She was intensely grateful when Bailey brought in the last of her things and she knew he would be leaving within moments, for she wasn't sure she could contain her tears any longer.

"Well, I guess it's all done, then," he said as he

stood at her front door, his hands jammed into his pockets.

"All's well that ends well. We both got what we wanted," she replied, willing him out the door. "I got pregnant..."

He smiled. "And I got saved from the wiles of deranged pageant contestants." His smile faltered and he pulled his hands from his pocket.

He raised a hand, and for a moment she thought he might reach out and capture one of her curls, or gently stroke down the side of her face. She stiffened, not wanting the touch, afraid it would be the undoing of her.

To her relief he dropped his arm to his side. "You'll call me tomorrow?"

"Of course," she replied. After all, it was important that they go back to doing what they did best— being best friends.

"Then I guess I'll talk to you tomorrow." He hesitated another moment on her front stoop, as if reluctant to leave her alone.

But she desperately needed to be alone. Her emotions were all over the charts, the overwhelming joy of knowing she was finally pregnant coupled with the devastating despair of her enormous love for Bailey.

"I'll talk to you tomorrow," she repeated, then with a forced bright smile she closed the door, severing their awkward parting.

She managed to stanch the tears that begged to be released by working for the next couple of hours. The items she'd packed and taken to Bailey's to enhance his house were returned to their rightful places in her apartment.

She hoped nobody had seen them moving her back in here. She wasn't ready for the questions she knew family and friends would have, at least not today. Tomorrow she'd talk to Bailey and they'd figure out exactly what they wanted to tell everyone.

She finished unpacking near dusk, then made herself some soup and sat at her kitchen table to eat. The silence of her apartment pressed around her with suffocating closeness.

The meals at Bailey's had always been accompanied by laughter and discussion and barking exclamations from Squirt. Tomato soup eaten alone and in utter silence couldn't compete.

She'd only eaten about half of the soup when the tears began. She'd gotten exactly what she'd wished for, but somehow in the space of the two months with Bailey, her wishes had changed.

She didn't just want Bailey's baby...she wanted Bailey. She wanted to see his beautiful face first thing in the mornings, fall asleep in his strong arms. She wanted to make love to him and raise babies with him and grow old with him. She wanted...

She shoved her bowl aside, a sob rising in her throat. The tears she'd held inside since that morning fell in a torrent. She stumbled from the table and into her bedroom, where she fell across the bed and buried her face in her pillow.

"Stop it," she said between sobs in an attempt to get control of herself. It wasn't as if she would never see Bailey again. He would forever be a part of her life as the father of her child. He would forever be a part of her life as her friend.

This thought only made her sob harder, for she knew the truth of things in her heart. She loved Bailey, but she'd made the horrifying mistake of falling in love with him. And she knew in her heart, knew in her soul, she could never go back to loving him just as a friend.

She'd not only lost the man that she loved, she'd lost her best friend.

Bailey awakened the next morning with Mellie's pillow wrapped tightly in his arms, the lingering scent of her perfume filling his head.

He threw the pillow aside and sat up, irritation winging through him. He needed to change the sheets. Mellie had become a habit in his life, and surely that's why it seemed so strange to awaken without her in his arms.

He rolled over on his back and stared up at the ceiling where the morning sun was sending fingers of light across the surface. He'd barely had time to assess all that had happened in the past twenty-four hours.

Mellie's pronouncement that she was pregnant and going back to her own place had stunned him, and things had moved far too quickly after that. After moving her things, he'd barely returned home when he'd received a phone call from Tanner Rothman with a foaling mare that was having difficulty.

It had been after midnight when he'd finally returned from the Rothman ranch, and he'd been vaguely surprised at his disappointment that Mellie wasn't there. He'd been revved up by the birth of the new foal, had wanted to share the excitement and joy with Mellie.

You can still do that, he told himself. She would call and he'd tell her all about it. Maybe he'd ask her if she wanted to meet him at the café for a burger this evening.

With this thought in mind, he bounded out of bed, pulled on a pair of jeans and padded into the kitchen to make coffee.

Although Squirt greeted him enthusiastically, the kitchen itself offered no warmth.

Without Mellie's pretty yellow place mats, towels and knickknacks, the kitchen looked sterile and impersonal.

"Just the way I like it," he muttered firmly. His house was his own again—a bachelor pad with no frilly, feminine items to distract him.

Still, minutes later as he ate his breakfast, he turned on the radio to fill the silence he'd never noticed in the house while Mellie was present.

"Just you and me, Squirt," he said, and forced a grin as Squirt's entire backside wiggled with pleasure.

"A man and his dog, that's exactly the way I was intended to live."

A habit. Throughout the afternoon Bailey told himself again that Mellie had just become a habit in his daily life, and that it sometimes took a little time to adjust when the habit was gone.

He worked with his animals and had appointments until noon, then went inside for lunch and checked his answering machine. No message from her.

He was halfway through his sandwich when Sam Johnson, a neighbor and friend, brought in his hunting dog. The dog had been hit by a car and needed immediate surgery to save his life.

Twilight was falling when Bailey finally made his way from the barn to the house. The dog, Neptune, had come through surgery fine and would be okay.

Bailey was exhausted, but it was the best kind of exhaustion, the kind that came with saving an animal's life. It was what Stephanie had never understood, and what Mellie had always understood.

Funny, he thought as he showered, how different the marriage experience had been with Mellie and Stephanie. With Stephanie he'd always felt lacking, inadequate and as if he would never measure up to the kind of man she wanted him to be. With Mellie he'd always been at peace with himself, had known he had her respect and approval.

After his shower, he checked his answering machine once again, surprised that there was still no call from Mellie. Sitting on the sofa with Squirt in his lap, he picked up his phone and called her place.

Her phone rang three times, then her answering machine picked up. He waited for the recording beep, then spoke. "Mellie...it's me. I guess you're out. Call me when you get in, okay?" He hung up, oddly unsettled by the fact that she hadn't called him all day long.

The next day he came in from his office to find a message from her. "Bailey," her voice said, "I just wanted to tell you that I think it best if we not mention my being pregnant right now. We can just tell our friends and our families that being good friends isn't enough to make a marriage and so we called it quits." There was a long pause, then she murmured a soft goodbye and the machine clicked off.

He tried to call her back, but once again got her machine. Over the next two days he tried to contact her, but always got the machine instead of her lively, beautiful voice.

By the time Friday arrived and he hadn't heard from her he began to worry. It wasn't like them to go so long without talking, without sharing a meal or two or meeting simply to talk, over a quick cup of coffee.

He paced his living room floor. He'd come in for lunch and had hoped, as he had every day for the past week, that there would be a message from her about their usual movie night. But there had been nothing.

What was going on with her? Was she sick? Was she having problems with the pregnancy? He tried to

tell himself that she was probably just busy reestab-
lishing her life in her apartment. She'd had boxes to
unload, clothes to hang and put away.

But surely she could have managed all that and still
found time for a phone call to him. He halted his
pacing as a thought occurred to him.

Surely the short-term marriage they'd shared hadn't
changed things between them. He absolutely, positively refused to consider that possibility.

They had made a deal, they'd both agreed that they
could get married, get Mellie pregnant, then go back
to the beautiful friendship that they both cherished.

He grabbed his truck keys and headed out the door.
It was time—past time—he got over to her place and
found out exactly what was going on.

Chapter Eleven

She knew the moment she heard the knock on her apartment door that it was Bailey. She didn't have to look through her peephole and see his face to know it was him.

"Mellie?"

She remained on the sofa, where she had been for most of the week. Maybe if she didn't answer he would go away. All week long she'd hoped she would get strong enough to talk to him on the phone, to see him in person, but she felt no stronger now than she had the first night here alone when she'd cried herself to sleep.

She hadn't realized how tightly woven he was into the fabric of her life, didn't realize the depth of depression that would settle over her when she contem-

plated life without his friendship, without his camaraderie, without his love.

He banged on the door again, this time louder. Her
car was parked out front, so he obviously knew she
was home. She stood, knowing she couldn't put off
the inevitable any longer. Sooner or later she was going to have to face him, and it might as well be now.

As she walked to the door, she attempted to smooth
her hair, which she knew must be in riotous disarray.
She opened the door to see his fist raised, apparently
preparing to knock yet again.

"There you are," he exclaimed. "I've been wondering if you're trying to avoid me."

"It's been a really busy week," she said as he
stepped into the living room.

He walked across the room and flopped down on
the sofa, as he'd done a million times before. Only
this time Melanie didn't see him as her best friend
and confidant, she saw him as the man she loved and
would never have, the man who had broken her heart.

As always he was clad in his jeans, the washed
denim hugging his long legs and displaying his slender hips and waist. The navy T-shirt stretched taut
across his broad chest, and there was nothing Melanie
wanted more than to sit next to him and lean into his
chest, smell the spicy scent of him, feel his strong
arms holding her tight.

She took the chair opposite the sofa, needing to
maintain physical distance from him, wondering how
long she could pretend that there was nothing wrong,

that there was no problem in returning to the relationship they'd had before their marriage.

"You said it's been a busy week. What have you been doing?"

She couldn't very well tell him she'd spent the past week drifting from room to room of her apartment like a robot and remembering every moment spent with him.

"This and that." She shrugged, knowing she was being vague. "It took me a couple of days to get this place back in order. After having it shut up for two months, I did some deep cleaning."

"Why didn't you call me? I could have helped."

For the first time in a week she felt the curve of a smile on her lips. "Bailey, no offense, but your idea of clean isn't quite the same as mine."

"I could have at least kept you company." His blue gaze held hers intently. "Are you coming over tonight for popcorn and movies?"

"I don't think so." She broke eye contact with him. "I'm tired. I think I'll stick around here and have an early night." She looked at him again to find him studying her. "Maybe next week," she added quickly.

He leaned forward and his eyes appeared to deepen in hue. "But next week the odds are good that you'll be too tired, too. And you'll probably be too busy to call or get together throughout the week. What's going on, Mellie?"

Again she found it too painful to gaze at him, to

hold eye contact. And she knew it wasn't fair of her not to be completely truthful with him.

"I can't, Bailey. I can't do this." The tremor in her voice horrified her.

"Do what?"

She heard the confusion in his voice, and she wanted to slap him for being obtuse. Couldn't he tell that everything had changed? Couldn't he feel her love for him filling this room at this very moment?

A flash of irritation mingled with the pain of her heartbreak. She stood, unable to sit still while she told him the final, most heart-wrenching secret of her life.

"Bailey, I can't do Friday movie nights with you anymore. I can't have coffee or go for walks or go swimming and hang out at your place."

She refused to look at him, but instead focused on the painting that hung over her sofa, above his head. "I love you, Bailey." The words, which when spoken should have brought her joy, instead sent a rivulet of grief flooding through her. Love was supposed to be the beginning of things, but in this case, Melanie knew it signified the end.

"I love you, too." His reply came instantaneously…automatically.

Despite the fact that she had cried for most of the week and had thought her tears completely depleted, her vision blurred with tears as she looked at him once again.

"You don't understand. I'm *in* love with you, Bailey." His eyes grew darker than she'd ever seen them and he opened his mouth to speak, but she hurriedly continued.

"I thought I could do this. I thought we could have a pretend marriage to get me pregnant, then we could go back to the friendship I cherished. But I was wrong." Tears burned her cheeks. "I can't go back to just being friends."

He stood, his features taut, and a spark of anger lit his eyes. "What are you talking about? This wasn't supposed to happen." He took a step toward her. "Dammit, Mellie, you didn't say anything about this happening."

She stared at him, stunned by his reaction. She'd expected him to be upset. She hadn't expected his obvious anger. "I didn't know it was going to happen," she exclaimed defensively. "I certainly didn't plan it."

"But you promised me nothing would change." His voice rose in volume with each word he spoke. "You knew I didn't want to be married ever again. You promised me we could do this and things would go back to the way they were—that was important to me."

"Don't yell at me," she said with a rising anger of her own. "You're acting like I did this on purpose, and I didn't. Trust me," she said bitterly, "the last thing I expected to happen was that I'd fall in love with you."

His eyes still blazed. "Well, can't you just get over it?"

For a moment she was left utterly speechless. She'd never before seen him so irrational. "This isn't a case of the flu or the measles, Bailey. I don't know if I can just 'get over it' or not."

"I can't believe you did this to me...to us."

Melanie's anger rose. "I told you I didn't want this to happen. I can't help the way I feel, so stop being such a jerk."

"If I'm such a jerk, then stop being in love with me and go back to being my friend."

She wanted to punch him for being stupid when it came to matters of the heart. She wanted to throw herself into his arms and make him hold her until her hurt went away.

Instead she drew a deep, weary breath and released it on a thick, heavy sigh. Again tears pressed at her eyes, the tears produced by the utter despair of her loss.

"Bailey, maybe time will make things better. I just don't know. But no matter what happens, I'll agree to joint custody of the baby."

He was still angry. She could tell by the taut set of his shoulders and the brisk, heavy footsteps that carried him to the front door. "Then I guess all that's left is for me to call you when I talk to a lawyer about the divorce."

He yanked open the front door and started out, but before he could get completely out he turned back to her, his eyes still sparking like an angry electrical fire. "If I had known the price we'd pay for our little scheme, I would never have agreed to it in the first place.'' He didn't wait for her reply, but turned and left, slamming the door behind him.

Melanie stared at the closed door for long moments, tears oozing unchecked from her eyes. She hadn't realized until this very moment that she'd still held on to a little bit of hope.

In the back of her mind she'd somehow believed that maybe if she confessed to Bailey that she was in love with him, he would suddenly recognize that he was in love with her. But that hadn't happened. Instead he'd been angry with her for screwing things up, for destroying their friendship.

For the first time since she'd been a skinny, red-haired, freckle-faced second-grader, she was going to have to live without Bailey in her life. She didn't even know how to begin.

Bailey couldn't even begin to describe all the emotions that warred inside him as he drove away from Mellie's apartment. He was angry with her for loving him, angry with himself for agreeing to the marriage in the first place.

His anger was tempered with deep regret and a bit of shame over how he had yelled at her moments before. Those beautiful green eyes of hers had been awash with tears, and her Cupid lips had trembled with the depth of her emotional turmoil.

But there was something else there besides the anger, another emotion aside from the regret and shame.

The idea that Mellie was lost to him and would no longer be an integral part of his everyday life filled him with grief…and fear.

The past week of not seeing her, of not talking to her, had been sheer torture, and now he realized it had merely been a prelude to the rest of their lives.

Oh, he would see her around town, interact with her about their child, but the sweet intimacy of their friendship, the utter trust and openness they'd always shared would be gone.

How was he going to survive without that? Nobody knew him the way she did. Nobody understood him the way she did. What was he going to do without her in his life?

He didn't know how long he drove, trying to clear his head, telling himself that he would be fine, that she would be fine. Hell, they'd just been friends, nothing more.

It was a little after five when he pulled into the driveway of his parents' house. He supposed it was time he break the news of his separation to them. He'd spoken with both his mother and his father through the week, but hadn't mentioned that Mellie had returned to her apartment in town.

He would also need to get the wedding gifts that were stored in his spare room back to the people who had bought them. Mellie had left him a detailed list of what went back to whom.

He shut off his truck engine and rubbed his forehead where a headache was attempting to take hold.

Mellie didn't want to tell anyone yet that she was pregnant, so he couldn't tell his mother that good news when he told her they were separated.

With a sigh he got out of his truck and headed for the house. He stepped through the front door and was surprised to be greeted by silence. Most evenings he'd find his parents here in the living room watching the early-evening news.

"Mom...Dad?" he called, then walked into the kitchen. It was obvious they'd had dinner not long before. The scent of his mother's meat loaf hung in the air, and several dishes were in the drainer dripping dry.

The back door was open, and as he approached the screen door he heard the faint murmur of their familiar voices and the creak of the porch swing.

He was about to open the door when he heard his mother giggle. It was a low, girlish sound he'd never heard from her before and it was followed by a long silence, then a sigh.

They were smooching. The thought struck him like a pit bull biting his midsection. His parents, the two people he'd thought were miserable with each other, were sweet-talking and kissing each other as the sun disappeared in the west.

Bailey backed away from the door and stealthily made his way back through the living room and out the front door. His thoughts raced as he got back into his truck and drove off in the direction of his own place.

For years Bailey had believed his parents were two miserable people trapped together by their marriage vows. Over and over again Mellie had tried to tell him that his parents' bickering and fussing with each other was good-natured, a form of foreplay.

But Bailey hadn't listened to her. He felt as if his entire world had been kicked out from under him, first by Mellie and now by the knowledge that his parents' marriage contained not only a lot of differences of opinion but apparently a love that had lasted through the years.

As he pulled in front of his house, his headache found a foothold and pounded across his forehead. He needed to go inside. He needed the peace and quiet of his house. He needed…he needed…hell, he had no idea what he needed.

Melanie had discovered in the past week that she hated sunset—that blurred time between day and night when it was too early to go to bed and too easy to fall into the purple gloom of the twilight.

And there was no gloom so deep and dark as that of a friendless one, she thought, as she sat at her kitchen table with a pad and a pencil in front of her and a cup of coffee within reach.

Tomorrow she positively, absolutely had to go grocery shopping. She'd spent the past week eating whatever canned goods had been in her pantry, not wanting to chance running into anyone in town. Now that she and Bailey had had their final parting of the ways, so to speak, she'd simply have to be prepared to tell anyone who might ask that they were separated and seeking a divorce.

It would be bad enough answering those questions now, but it would be far worse when a few months had passed and her pregnancy started to show.

Her pregnancy. She placed her hands on her abdomen, thinking of the baby growing inside. Despite her anguish over Bailey and how things had turned out, she wasn't sorry about the baby. Rather she was thrilled. She would always have a piece of Bailey in her life—his little girl or little boy to love and cherish.

She got up from the sofa and headed for the bedroom, deciding it was okay to get into her pajamas before 7:00 p.m. She'd just entered her bedroom when she heard a knock on her door. Who could that be?

She didn't think anyone knew she was here. Maybe one of her friends or a neighbor had seen a light on in here and was checking up on things.

Apparently the time for answering nosy questions had come. Wearily she left the bedroom and went to the front door. She gasped in surprise as she saw Bailey standing there.

"I know you said you didn't want to see me anymore," he began without preamble.

"I didn't exactly say I didn't want to see you anymore," she returned, irritated that her voice sounded uneven and fragile.

"I need you to come with me, Mellie."

"Come with you where?" She held the door tightly, as if that would not only keep him out of her home but also out of her heart.

"Back to my place. It's Squirt."

Melanie's heart fell. "Squirt? What's wrong? Is he hurt?" She grabbed Bailey's hand in a painfully tight squeeze, tears leaping into her eyes.

"No...no," he said hurriedly. "It's nothing real bad. He...he just isn't eating. I think he misses you. I thought maybe you could come out and visit with him for a few minutes and get him to eat."

Although the last place she wanted to be was at Bailey's, where memories of loving him could only torture her, she couldn't ignore Squirt's needs.

"All right, I'll come for just a little while," she agreed. "Jut let me grab my purse."

A few moments later she was seated next to Bailey in his truck, the scent of him whirling in the air with a familiarity that ached inside her.

After making love with Bailey for a week or two, she'd worried that she might be a nymphomaniac be-cause she'd believed it was the sex that she liked so much. But it had been making love to Bailey that she liked, and the thought of making love with any other man was repugnant.

She shot a surreptitious glance at Bailey, who was humming just under his breath. Humming...which meant he had something on his mind. There was a time when she would have been able to guess what he was thinking about or concentrating on, but no more.

He must have felt her gaze on him. He glanced at her quickly, then back out the window. "I'm sorry I was a jerk earlier," he said.

She wanted to be angry with him. Anger would make it so much easier to deal with him. But she couldn't sustain any anger. She'd never been able to stay mad at him.

"It's all right," she said softly. "We both got rather emotional."

They fell into a silence. The silence wasn't the companionable kind they once enjoyed, but rather an uncomfortable quiet that begged to be broken.

But Melanie had nothing more to say. She'd said everything earlier to him, and apparently he'd said all he needed to then, as well.

So the silence grew, and in its wake Melanie's heartbreak built once again to a near crescendo. She stared blankly out the window, her heart wrapped in pain as he turned down the lane that led to his house.

The sun had set, and dark shadows had taken up residency, but his porch light burned bright, illuminating the porch and the swing that had never been there before.

As he pulled the truck to a halt, she turned to stare at him, remembering that he'd told her the day he got a porch swing would be the day he'd be declared insane.

"You've lost your mind?" she asked softly.

He shut off the engine, unbuckled his seat belt, then turned to face her. "I have."

"Is this what you brought me out here to show me?" She didn't understand what the swing implied, why he had bought one. Was this some crazy attempt to apologize for yelling at her earlier? Was it some misguided effort to make her be friends with him once again?

"Let's get out and have a swing. I have a few things to tell you," he said.

How cruel could he be? Didn't he realize part of her fantasy had been the two of them sitting in a swing, watching their children play in the yard? Didn't he realize she'd dreamed of sitting on a porch swing with him each evening, sharing the events of the day, sharing the passion of their hearts?

Still, even knowing it would be torture, she got out of the truck and followed him up to the porch. He waited until she was seated in the swing, then he eased down next to her, his thigh warm and firm against hers.

"Mellie, from the time I left your place this afternoon I've been doing a lot of thinking. I drove for hours, angry that things had turned out the way they had." He drew a deep breath and set the swing moving to and fro.

"I finally stopped at my parents' place. I'd decided it was time for me to tell them that we were separated." He didn't look at her, but rather stared off in the distance before them.

"What did they say?" She knew how difficult it must have been for him, knew she would be facing the same difficulty when she spoke to her parents.

"I never got a chance to talk to them." He turned to look at her. "When I got there, they were on the back porch, sitting in the swing and making out like a couple of teenagers."

Despite everything, to Melanie's surprise a giggle escaped her lips. "Henry and Luella making out?"

Bailey grinned wryly. "I know, just the thought of it might leave me scarred for life." His smile fell and he reached up and swept a hand through his hair. "I left before they realized I was there. I was so stunned to realize they obviously love each other...that it's love that has kept them together."

"I've been trying to tell you that for years," Melanie chided.

"Yeah, but I never really got it until today. My parents are best friends and oftentimes the worst of enemies, but at the end of each day they come together to share tenderness and caring and passion. They're friends and lovers."

Melanie tensed, wondering if what he was getting at was that he still wanted the divorce, but he wanted not only friendship privileges with her but sex as well. "Bailey, if you think..."

"Shh, let me finish. That's your problem, Mellie, you're always rambling on about something or another when a guy has something important to say."

He smiled at her, a smile that threatened to steal her breath away.

"You know how I've always felt about being an only child. No kid should be an only child," he continued. "And I sure don't want my kid to be an only child."

"Bailey, you're the one doing the rambling," she exclaimed in frustration. "For goodness sake, tell me what I'm doing here."

His gaze held hers intently. "I told you when we first pulled up and you saw this swing that I'd lost my mind. I lost it when I thought of a life without you."

He grabbed her hand and wrapped his fingers tightly...warmly around it. "I thought back over all the years we've known each other. I thought about the fact that whenever I felt lonely or sad or happy or scared, you were always the one I wanted around me."

She gazed at him, his handsome face, his beautiful eyes, and her heart beat just a little faster in her chest as she listened to what he had to say. But for the first time she could ever remember, she was afraid to guess where, exactly, he was going with it all.

"When I graduated from college, Mellie, it was your face, not Stephanie's, that I looked for in the audience. Stephanie was supposed to be the woman I loved, but it was your freckled face I most wanted to see."

He released her hand and instead stroked a finger

down her cheek. "Skinny, minny Mellie, I realized today that I've been in love with you since the second grade and I don't want a divorce and I don't want to spend one minute of my life without you in it."

Melanie stared at him...afraid to believe, afraid that somehow her sense of hearing was playing tricks on her. "If this is one of your sick jokes, Bailey, I'll never, ever forgive you," she finally said.

"When have I ever played a sick joke on you?" he asked indignantly.

"In sixth grade when you slipped worms into my sandwich, then bet Mike Moore that I could eat mine faster than he could eat his. Thankfully I saw the worms before I took the first bite."

Bailey's eyes lit merrily. "Okay, so I've played a sick joke on you before...but that was when we were kids." He sobered and his eyes grew darker. "We aren't kids anymore, Mellie. I want to be your best friend, but I also want to be your husband, the man you build dreams with and sit on porch swings with...I want to be the man you make love to every night for the rest of your life."

"Oh, Bailey, if you don't kiss me this very moment I swear I'm going to die," she cried.

He complied, drawing her into his arms and kissing her with such a sweet tenderness that every broken piece of her heart came back together in joy.

When the kiss ended, she looked at him solemnly. "Bailey, this isn't about the baby, is it? I mean, you aren't just staying married to me so that we can have another baby and we won't have an only child?''

"My sweet Mellie, there's only one thing that could make me remain married to you, and that's love. And I'm not talking about the love of a friend for a friend, I'm talking about the love of one soul mate for another. You are my soul mate, you know.''

She nodded, momentarily too filled with emotion to speak.

"I think I was in love with you when I beat up Harley Raymond in the fifth grade for you.''

She laughed and shook her head. "Harley beat the tar out of you, but it was the thought that counted.''

He captured her face in his hands, his eyes caressing her with a heat that was tangible. "No, Mellie, it's the love that counted. And I want to spend the rest of my days loving you and being in love with you.''

His mouth captured hers again. This time his kiss tasted of the trust and laughter of friendship, the passionate desire of a lover and the lifetime commitment of a soul mate.

"I love you, Mellie,'' he whispered softly against her ear.

"And I love you, Bailey,'' she replied.

He stood abruptly, and she squealed as he picked her up in his arms. "What are you doing?'' she asked.

"Doing what I should have done two months ago,'' he replied. "Some things just need to be done right to stick, and I figure if I carry you over the threshold all proper-like, then that makes our marriage real and forever.''

Real and forever. The words echoed inside her, wrapping her heart with happiness. ''You might be the judge of the Miss Dairy Cow Contest, Bailey Jenkins, but when you look at me the way you're looking at me right now, I feel like I'm the queen of the Miss Dairy Cow Contest.''

He laughed, his eyes burning into hers with a blaze of love and desire. ''One thing is for sure—you're the queen of my heart.'' With these words he kicked open the front door and carried his wife over the threshold.

*   *   *   *   *

MILLS & BOON®

Live the emotion

FEBRUARY 2004 HARDBACK TITLES

ROMANCE™

The Mistress Purchase Penny Jordan   H5940   0 263 18219 3
The Outback Marriage Ransom Emma Darcy
   H5941   0 263 18220 7
A Spanish Marriage Diana Hamilton   H5942   0 263 18221 5
His Virgin Secretary Cathy Williams   H5943   0 263 18222 3
The Italian's Secret Child Catherine Spencer
   H5944   0 263 18223 1
The Greek Millionaire's Marriage Sara Wood
   H5945   0 263 18224 X
In Her Boss's Bed Maggie Cox   H5946   0 263 18225 8
The Italian's Suitable Wife Lucy Monroe   H5947   0 263 18226 6
The Duke's Proposal Sophie Weston   H5948   0 263 18227 4
Princess in the Outback Barbara Hannay   H5949   0 263 18228 2
Marriage in Name Only Barbara McMahon   H5950   0 263 18229 0
A Professional Engagement Darcy Maguire
   H5951   0 263 18230 4
If the Stick Turns Pink... Carla Cassidy   H5952   0 263 18231 2
Pregnant by the Boss! Carol Grace   H5953   0 263 18232 0
The Greek Children's Doctor Sarah Morgan   H5954   0 263 18233 9
Surgeon in Crisis Jennifer Taylor   H5955   0 263 18234 7

HISTORICAL ROMANCE™

My Lady English Catherine March   H569   0 263 18397 1
A Most Unsuitable Bride Gail Whitiker   H570   0 263 18398 X

MEDICAL ROMANCE™

Doctor at Risk Alison Roberts   M487   0 263 18421 8
The Doctor's Outback Baby Carol Marinelli
   M488   0 263 18422 6

MILLS & BOON®

Live the emotion

FEBRUARY 2004 LARGE PRINT TITLES

ROMANCE™

Mistress for a Month Miranda Lee	1647	0 263 18043 3
In Separate Bedrooms Carole Mortimer	1648	0 263 18044 1
The Italian's Love-Child Sharon Kendrick	1649	0 263 18045 X
The Greek's Virgin Bride Julia James	1650	0 263 18046 8
Outback Bridegroom Margaret Way	1651	0 263 18047 6
The Forbidden Marriage Rebecca Winters	1652	0 263 18048 4
The Boss's Convenient Proposal Barbara McMahon		
	1653	0 263 18049 2
Their Accidental Baby Hannah Bernard	1654	0 263 18050 6

HISTORICAL ROMANCE™

Colonel Ancroft's Love Sylvia Andrew	267	0 263 18181 2
One Night With a Rake Louise Allen	268	0 263 18182 0

MEDICAL ROMANCE™

The Pregnancy Proposition Meredith Webber		
	497	0 263 18135 9
A White Knight in ER Jessica Matthews	498	0 263 18136 7
The Surgeon's Child Alison Roberts	499	0 263 18137 5
Dr Marco's Bride Carol Wood	500	0 263 18138 3

MILLS & BOON®

Live the emotion

MARCH 2004 HARDBACK TITLES

ROMANCE™

The Stephanides Pregnancy Lynne Graham

	H5956	0 263 18235 5
The Passion Price Miranda Lee	H5957	0 263 18236 3
The Sultan's Bought Bride Jane Porter	H5958	0 263 18237 1
The Deserving Mistress Carole Mortimer	H5959	0 263 18238 X
The South American's Wife Kay Thorpe	H5960	0 263 18239 8
A Latin Passion Kathryn Ross	H5961	0 263 18240 1
Reclaiming His Bride Margaret Mayo	H5962	0 263 18241 X
The Greek Boss's Demand Trish Morey	H5963	0 263 18242 8
The Takeover Bid Leigh Michaels	H5964	0 263 18243 6
A Marriage Worth Waiting For Susan Fox	H5965	0 263 18244 4
The Pregnant Tycoon Caroline Anderson	H5966	0 263 18245 2

The Honeymoon Proposal Hannah Bernard

	H5967	0 263 18246 0
Caught by Surprise Sandra Paul	H5968	0 263 18247 9
The Cinderella Inheritance Carolyn Zane	H5969	0 263 18248 7

The Doctor's Unexpected Family Lilian Darcy

	H5970	0 263 18249 5
The English Doctor's Baby Sarah Morgan	H5971	0 263 18250 9

HISTORICAL ROMANCE™

A Very Unusual Governess Sylvia Andrew	H571	0 263 18399 8
A Convenient Gentleman Victoria Aldridge	H572	0 263 18400 5

MEDICAL ROMANCE™

His Pregnant GP Lucy Clark	M489	0 263 18423 4
A Father's Special Care Gill Sanderson	M490	0 263 18424 2

MARCH 2004 LARGE PRINT TITLES

ROMANCE™

HISTORICAL ROMANCE™

MEDICAL ROMANCE™